Check your e-
information abo

The message was signed *MysteryMom*.

"Huh." Elise shifted on her chair and cast a glance to Jared. "What do you suppose…?"

He shrugged. "Check your e-mail." While she navigated to a new webpage and accessed her e-mail account, he pulled his chair closer to the desk so that he was beside her.

She opened the e-mail and leaned closer to the screen to read.

Dear Elise, I read your post to the "Parents Without Children" message board with a heavy heart. Losing a child is every mother's worst nightmare, and the last thing I'd ever want is to add to your pain. But the circumstances of your story rang familiar to me, and I took the liberty of doing some digging. I have powerful contacts with access to reliable information about birth records and have made it my mission to help mothers like you—and I do think I can help you. Not wanting to raise false hope for you, I triple-checked my information before contacting you.

Elise, my sources tell me that your baby might be alive.

Dear Reader,

Last autumn, I was brainstorming story ideas centered around babies and hunky heroes when my agent let me know that the editors at Intrigue had asked if I wanted to write a story for the TOP SECRET DELIVERIES series. I would be free to write whatever story I wanted as long as I incorporated MysteryMom, the behind-the-scenes woman who has been helping reunite parents with their babies in earlier books in the series. Call it fate, or serendipity, or just good luck, but all the pieces came together in the right place and time. "As a matter of fact," I told my agent, "I have been working on a story that fits those parameters beautifully. Count me in!"

I hope you enjoy Elise and Jared's love story, one in which fate/serendipity/good luck gets a helping hand from MysteryMom, and tragedy leads to the sweetest blessings...love and family.

Thank you to Tammy Yenalavitch of Charlotte, North Carolina, for sharing her kitties, Bubba, Diva and Brooke with me for this story. Tammy won the chance to have her cats featured in my book through a contest I ran on Facebook. Stay tuned, more chances to win fame and celebrity for *your* cat will be coming soon!

Best wishes and happy reading,

Beth

OPERATION BABY RESCUE

BY
BETH CORNELISON

All the characters in this book have no existence outside the imagination of the author, and have no relation whatsoever to anyone bearing the same name or names. They are not even distantly inspired by any individual known or unknown to the author, and all the incidents are pure invention.

All Rights Reserved including the right of reproduction in whole or in part in any form. This edition is published by arrangement with Harlequin Enterprises II B.V./S.à.r.l. The text of this publication or any part thereof may not be reproduced or transmitted in any form or by any means, electronic or mechanical, including photocopying, recording, storage in an information retrieval system, or otherwise, without the written permission of the publisher.

This book is sold subject to the condition that it shall not, by way of trade or otherwise, be lent, resold, hired out or otherwise circulated without the prior consent of the publisher in any form of binding or cover other than that in which it is published and without a similar condition including this condition being imposed on the subsequent purchaser.

® and ™ are trademarks owned and used by the trademark owner and/or its licensee. Trademarks marked with ® are registered with the United Kingdom Patent Office and/or the Office for Harmonisation in the Internal Market and in other countries.

First published in Great Britain 2012
by Mills & Boon, an imprint of Harlequin (UK) Limited,
Eton House, 18-24 Paradise Road, Richmond, Surrey TW9 1SR

© Beth Cornelison 2011

ISBN: 978 0 263 89528 5
ebook ISBN: 978 1 408 97734 7

946-0512

Harlequin (UK) policy is to use papers that are natural, renewable and recyclable products and made from wood grown in sustainable forests. The logging and manufacturing processes conform to the legal environmental regulations of the country of origin.

Printed and bound in Spain
by Blackprint CPI, Barcelona

Beth Cornelison started writing stories as a child when she penned a tale about the adventures of her cat, Ajax. A Georgia native, she received her bachelor's degree in public relations from the University of Georgia. After working in public relations for a little more than a year, she moved with her husband to Louisiana, where she decided to pursue her love of writing fiction.

Since that first time, Beth has written many more stories of adventure and romance suspense and has won numerous honors for her work, including a coveted Golden Heart award in romance suspense from Romance Writers of America. She is active on the board of directors for the North Louisiana Storytellers and Authors of Romance (NOLA STARS) and loves reading, traveling, Peanuts' Snoopy and spending downtime with her family.

She writes from her home in Louisiana, where she lives with her husband, one son and two cats who think they are people. Beth loves to hear from her readers. You can write to her at PO Box 5418, Bossier City, LA 71171, USA or visit her website, www.bethcornelison.com.

To my mom, who is always ready to lend me a helping hand (or eyes to read a manuscript) and who shares my passion for books. I love you!

Prologue

"Push!"

Elise Norris squeezed her eyes shut, gritted her teeth and pushed through the contraction that wrenched her belly in an excruciating vise grip.

The nurse at her side held her hand and wiped perspiration from Elise's brow. "You're doing great! Almost there…"

"Now breathe. Catch your breath. I think the next one should do it." Dr. Arrimand peered at her over his mask and gave a confident nod.

As the pain eased, Elise rolled her head to the side to gaze at the ultrasound image of her daughter that was taped to the bed rail. The photo, which she'd carried in her wallet for weeks, had been her focal point throughout the delivery. In fact, her daughter had been her focal point for the past nine months. Longer than that. She'd been planning for, saving money for and praying for this day for years.

With a trembling finger, she traced the lines of the fuzzy picture she'd memorized in the past several weeks and smiled. Raising a child alone would be difficult. She had no illusions otherwise. But Elise had known she wanted to be a mother, wanted to raise a family, since she'd been a little girl herself. When she'd celebrated her thirtieth birthday without a husband with whom she could share the joys of parenthood, she'd researched sperm banks and set about finding the perfect donor to father her baby.

"It's okay, Gracie," she whispered to the ultrasound picture. "We'll be fine. You and me. We'll be a t-team." The last word of her pledge caught in her throat as another powerful spasm of pain ripped through her. Building quickly to a crescendo, the contraction stole her breath.

"This is it. Keep pushing!" Dr. Arrimand coached.

She clenched her teeth and concentrated on bringing her daughter into the world. All her physical strength and love were focused on the task. Minutes later, the nurse laid a pink-faced bundle in her arms.

Elise gazed into her daughter's eyes and fell instantly in love. The bond was powerful, emotional, solid. Her daughter. Her flesh and blood. Her dream come true.

With one finger she traced Gracie's nose and lips. "Hi, sweetheart. I'm your mommy. Oh, you're beautiful." She smoothed her daughter's tiny eyebrows and kissed her sweet forehead. A thin layer of hair the same shade of golden blond as Elise's crowned Grace's head, and she saw her own blue eyes reflected in her baby's cerulean gaze. "You're perfect. I love you."

Elise tugged on the pink blanket the nurse had swaddled Gracie in and freed her daughter's right arm. She lifted Grace's hand and studied the tiny fingers, perfect fingernails, delicate skin. "So sweet and little…"

Not wanting Grace to get chilled, Elise pulled the

blanket back around her daughter and noticed a small red pear-shaped birthmark on Grace's right shoulder. "Angel kissed," she whispered to Grace. "That's what my mom said about my brother's birthmark."

A pang of regret stung her heart. Had she lived, what would her mother have thought about her granddaughter, her namesake?

At her side, the nurse fumbled with the tubes of her IV.

"What's that?" she asked, spotting the syringe in the nurse's hand.

"This will help with the pain so you can rest." She injected a clear solution into the port and smiled. "Just another minute, Mom, then I need to take the baby to be checked thoroughly by the staff pediatrician."

Already the drug she'd been given made Elise woozy. She frowned. She hadn't asked for pain medicine. She wanted to be alert, savoring every detail of the experience. "I don't want to sleep. I want to be with my baby, to bond…"

She heard her speech slur slightly as her eyelids drooped.

"We'll bring her to your room later to breastfeed." The nurse scooped Grace from Elise's arms, and Elise felt a pang in her heart.

"Not yet. Give me… just another… minute." But Elise could barely keep her eyes open. She forced herself to stay awake long enough to watch the nurse whisk Grace through the door to the next room. As she disappeared from Elise's line of sight, her daughter gave a mewling cry.

Gracie…

Elise fought off the fog of sleep and blinked her surroundings into focus. The patient room at the small-town hospital was not lavishly furnished but was comfortable and painted a cheerful pale yellow. With a sigh she thought of the state-of-the-art hospital in Lagniappe, Louisiana, where she'd planned to give birth.

With her due date still three weeks away, she'd believed she'd be fine driving to the weekend crafts fair in the rural community forty-five minutes from her home. If she began having contractions, she could easily get back to Lagniappe. Or so she'd thought. But the best laid plans…

Her water had broken while she paid for an antique rocking chair, and the contractions had come hard and fast. Within ten miles, she'd been doubled over in pain and had pulled to the side of the road to call 911.

The local ambulance had arrived quickly—thank God—and she'd been rushed to Pine Mill Community Hospital in time for the delivery.

The window was dark now, telling her night had fallen, and she searched her walls for a clock. How long had she slept? A simple white clock over the door read eleven forty-five. Elise rubbed her eyes and worked to clear the cobwebs of drug-induced sleep to do the simple calculation. Grace had been born at 3:30 p.m., so…more than eight hours had passed. She groaned and found the call button on the bed rail.

Enough of sleep. She wanted to hold her daughter. Nurse her daughter. Memorize every inch of her daughter's face and hands and toes…

"Can I help you?" came the response to her page.

"I'm awake now, and I want to see my baby. Can someone bring her to me?"

Her request met silence then a hesitant, "Um, I'll…have the doctor come talk to you."

The doctor? Elise tensed, butterflies kicking to life in

her gut. She didn't like the uneasy hesitation in the nurse's voice.

"Is there a problem? Is my baby okay?"

"Dr. Arrimand will be in to see you in a moment, ma'am," a different, more authoritative voice said.

"But what about my daughter? I want to see her." No response. "Hello? Hello? I want my baby brought to me!"

Again silence answered her. She buzzed the nurses' station, but her page was ignored. Irritation and concern spiked her pulse. Elise threw back her covers and swung her feet to the floor.

If they wouldn't bring Grace to her, she'd go get her from the nursery herself. She was Grace's mother, and they had no right to keep her from her. If something was wrong, she deserved answers…now!

Her head spun as she pushed off the bed, and her body throbbed from the rigors of the delivery. Elise grabbed the bed railing to keep from falling. Black spots danced in front of her eyes, and she waited impatiently for her equilibrium to return. When the room stopped shifting around her, she tried again to make her way to the door.

"Oh, Ms. Norris! You shouldn't try to walk alone yet!" a nurse fussed as she bustled into the room with a blood-pressure cuff in her hands. She took Elise's elbow and steered her back to the bed.

Elise tried to shrug away from the nurse's grip. "I want to see my daughter!"

With a strength that overpowered Elise's post-delivery condition, the nurse guided her back to the bed. "Dr. Arrimand has been called. He's on his way, and he'll explain everything."

The cryptic response rang warning bells in her head. A bubble of panic formed in her chest. "What does he have to explain? What's wrong with Grace?"

"The doctor will—"

"No! Tell me now! What happened? Where's my baby?" Tremors of dread shook her.

At that moment, the dark haired doctor, now wearing a white lab coat instead of scrubs, stepped into her room and helped the nurse maneuver Elise back to the bed.

Elise drilled the doctor with a hard, frantic stare. "Where's my daughter? Why won't anyone talk to me?"

Dr. Arrimand took a step back from the side of the bed and cleared his throat. "I'm sorry, Ms. Norris, but while you were asleep, your daughter's heart…" He paused, pressing his mouth in a grim line, then sighed heavily. "…Stopped beating."

A chill washed through Elise, and she was sure her heart had stopped, as well. "Wh—what?"

"We did everything we could to resuscitate her, but… we couldn't save her."

The room tilted. Blood whooshed in her ears. Shock rendered her mute and unable to move.

This couldn't be happening. She had to be hallucinating from the drugs they'd given her. Surely she'd heard him wrong. They had the wrong person.

"I'm very sorry," the doctor muttered, eyeing her with pity.

No. Her baby was *not* dead.

No, no, no, no, noooo!

The denials in her head became a keening wail. Agony and horror rose in a suffocating wave, filling her chest, squeezing her throat.

Questions pounded her brain. What made her heart stop? Why couldn't they save her? Why had they waited to tell her? Where was Grace now?

But her heart ached too much to voice them. Shock

and grief made all but gasping sobs and tormented moans beyond her reach.

In the blink of an eye, her dream come true had turned into every parent's worst nightmare. Her baby was dead.

Chapter 1

Fourteen months later

Elise shuffled into the church fellowship hall and cast a wary gaze around the assembled group. The rich aroma of freshly brewed coffee scented the air, lending a warmth and welcome to what she expected to be a most uncomfortable environment—sharing her grief with strangers.

One of the women seated in the circle of chairs spotted her standing in the doorway and called to her. "Hello. Are you looking for the grief-support meeting?"

Elise took a reinforcing breath and nodded.

The woman stood and waved her closer. "Please, come join us." As Elise approached the circle of chairs, several of the men stood, as well, greeting her with smiles and nods of welcome, and the woman who'd spoken first took her hand and patted it. "My name's Joleen Causey. I'm the group facilitator. Welcome."

"Thanks. I'm Elise Norris." She gave Joleen an awkward smile, and when the facilitator motioned to a seat next to her, Elise sat on the folding metal chair. As the others introduced themselves in an onslaught of names she didn't even try to remember, she scanned the faces of the group gathered in the small circle and gripped the edge of her chair. Several elderly ladies gave her curious glances, two gentlemen with gray-streaked hair nodded in greeting, a couple about her age clutched hands and sent her wan smiles, and a raven-haired man she estimated to be in his early thirties met her gaze and flashed her a strained crooked grin. "Jared Coleman," he said.

Other than the couple who clung to each other's hands as if their lives depended on it, Jared Coleman stood out simply because he was at least twenty-five years younger than any of the other members. She wondered briefly whom he'd lost and how he'd wound up in this group.

She'd been told about the group by a neighbor who attended the church that sponsored the meetings. For six months, Elise had worked on gathering the nerve to attend this grief-support program. For someone who'd been looking out for herself most of her life, who had established her independence from an early age and prided herself on her efficiency, reliability and self-sufficiency, seeking help had felt like a defeat. But when the one-year anniversary of Grace's death passed, Elise had still been moving through her life in the same fog of pain and denial as she had the first week. While she knew she'd never forget the child she lost, she had to come to grips with Grace's death so she could move on in her life.

"Don't feel like you have to talk tonight if all you want to do is listen," Joleen said. "But if you want to talk about what brought you here today or anything else that's in your heart, please feel free. We're here to listen and support you however we can." She flashed another warm and encouraging smile, tucking a wisp of her blond hair behind her ear, and Elise nodded.

"I came tonight because…" She took a deep breath. "…Just over a year ago, my daughter died right after birth."

Across the circle, the young wife gasped. Elise's gaze darted to her, but the woman was sharing a sad look with her husband. A prick of envy poked Elise. At least this woman had someone to share her grief with. In the past months, Elise had felt more alone than ever.

Elise squeezed her hands into such tight fists, her fingernails bit into her palms. "I only had a few minutes to hold her before…" She paused, feeling a knot forming in her throat. "Anyway, I'm just having a hard time… handling it."

"Of course. Many people say losing a child is the hardest death for a person to experience. But you're not alone." Joleen gestured to the rest of the group. "We're all here to help each other."

Elise forced a thin smile of acknowledgment then stared down at her lap. She hadn't talked with anyone about Gracie in months, largely because she couldn't get through even a simple comment without getting choked up. And the instant her eyes got teary, her neighbors or her colleagues at the Lagniappe newspaper, where she was a staff photographer, would back away with stricken expressions, as if they expected her to dissolve into wailing histrionics.

Knowing that her grief made other people uncomfortable chafed. Since when was there a time limit on compassion for a person's loss? But since talking about Grace was difficult anyway, she'd soon learned to avoid the topic of her daughter. Would sharing her feelings about Grace and the unfairness of her loss be any easier here?

"We lost our baby, too."

Elise jerked her head up and looked at the man who sat clinging to his wife.

The wife had her mouth pressed in a tight line as if struggling not to cry, but her eyes held Elise's. In an even tone, the husband continued, "It's been six months now, and while coming here—" he gestured with his head to the group "—has helped, it's still hard, really hard, for both of us to deal with. So while I won't pretend to know what you are feeling, because everyone grieves differently, we know at least something of what you're going through."

The wife bit her bottom lip and nodded to Elise.

"My son Sammy died fifteen years ago," a white-haired lady next to Elise said, patting her arm, "and I still think of him every day. It gets easier with time, but a mother's love never ends."

Elise swallowed hard, fighting back the stranglehold of emotion rising in her throat. If she allowed her tears to come now, she was afraid she might not be able to stop crying. Had coming here been a mistake? How could she relive the horror of that day, the crushing sense of loss over and again by coming to this group every week?

When she scanned the faces around the circle again, her gaze met Jared Coleman's. His dark brown eyes were locked on her, and an odd expression of guilt or uneasiness shadowed his face.

"Do you and your husband have any other children?" Joleen asked, and it took a moment for Elise to realize the question was directed to her.

"Oh, I...I'm not married. And no, no other children."

Joleen gave her a sympathetic look. "I see. Well, the loss of a child can be hard on a marriage. Divorce, sadly, is common following such a tragedy."

The young woman across the circle nodded. "Greg and

I have promised each other to be open and honest about our feelings. This group is part of our strategy to make sure our marriage survives."

Elise shook her head. "No, I mean I was never married. I—" Elise stopped when the eyebrow of one of the older women across from her raised in judgment. She didn't owe this group an explanation of her personal choices. A pulse of anger for the woman's haughty attitude helped Elise get a handle on the burgeoning tears in her throat. Taking a deep restorative breath, she folded her arms around her midriff and sat back in her chair. She stared at the floor near her feet, second-guessing her decision to attend the meeting.

Joleen apparently read Elise's body language for what it was, a disinclination to say any more on the topic, and directed the next question elsewhere.

"Jared, earlier you mentioned that you'd had an especially tough day last week. Would you like to tell us what happened?"

Without raising her head, Elise angled her gaze up from the floor to glance at Jared Coleman. He met her eyes briefly before clearing his throat, shrugging a shoulder dismissively and shifting in his seat. "Um, I…" His gaze darted away, and he cracked the knuckles of one hand with his other.

His restlessness and reluctance to speak intrigued Elise. Especially since his guilty furtive glances toward her told her his discomfort sharing with the group centered on her presence. She made a point of averting her gaze, hoping to make him feel less on the spot.

"Isabel took her first steps last Wednesday," Jared said at last.

Around the circle, several of the women cooed.

Elise tightened her grip on her sleeves. First steps? Clearly Isabel was a baby. About one year old.

The same age Grace would have been had she lived.

Like a fist to the gut, a shot of renewed grief landed a sucker punch that stole Elise's breath. She sat very still, keeping her gaze on the floor, but she felt Jared's eyes watching her.

"As happy as I was about her walking," he continued, "it just brought home to me, again, all the milestones Kelly will never see."

Now the women around the circle made noises of empathy and shared sadness for Jared's revelation.

Elise made a few mental calculations. Jared was here alone. He apparently had a one-year-old daughter. Was the absent Kelly his wife?

He said no more about the situation, letting his feelings about the event go unspoken. In the ensuing silence, one of the older women launched into a story about missing her late husband during the holidays and family celebrations.

Elise hazarded a glace across the circle and found Jared's attention on her again. Instead of jerking her gaze away, as if she'd been caught peeking at something forbidden, she held his stare. More than grief over the story he'd just shared, she saw concern and guilt in his dark brown eyes. Guilt?

She was still pondering the reason behind his odd expression half an hour later when the group dismissed for refreshments. Elise had no appetite for the cookies on the table by the exit, but her mouth was dry, and she decided to stop for a cup of lemonade before she left. Her pause at the refreshment table gave Joleen a chance to catch up with her before Elise made her escape from the awkward meeting.

"I'm so glad you came tonight," she said, placing a hand on Elise's arm. "I hope you'll come back. Talking about your experiences and your feelings gets easier with practice, and having the support of people who understand what you're going through is invaluable."

How could anyone really know what she was feeling? Her grief seemed so personal.

Elise forced a smile. "Thank you." She made no comment on whether she'd return. The jury was still out on that. Even the little she'd said tonight had been painful to share. She drained her lemonade quickly, hoping to make a hasty exit before any other members of the group caught her in an uncomfortable conversation. Tossing her empty cup in the trash, she spun on her heel to leave...and almost collided with a broad chest belonging to a man with dark brown, soulful eyes.

"Hi," Jared said with a quick flash of a lopsided grin.

"Oh, uh...hi." Elise's heartbeat performed a stutter-step. He was much taller than she'd expected, and this close to him, she could smell a tantalizing hint of sandalwood.

He rubbed his palms on his jeans once before sliding his hands in his pockets. The rattle of keys told her he was fidgeting. "I'm sorry if I...made you uneasy or caused you more pain tonight."

She blinked at him and furrowed her brow. She wasn't sure what she'd expected him to say, but an apology was not on the list. "Pardon?"

"Talking about my daughter." He gave an apologetic wince. "When the Harrisons joined the group..." He hitched his head toward the young couple still chatting with an older lady at the circle of chairs. "...Kim would get upset when I talked about Isabel. I thought, maybe, since you'd lost your baby...hearing about my daughter would be…especially difficult." He pressed his lips in a taut line of regret. "If it was, I'm sorry."

Elise could only stare for a moment. His sensitivity to her pain was thoughtful and also…frustrating.

"I, um…" She shook her head in disbelief. "Thank you, but…I don't expect you to censor yourself to protect me. Sure, it hurts to hear about other people's kids and think about what might have been, but…that's not your problem."

He shrugged and frowned. "Maybe, but I'd hate to think you decided not to come back because my stories about Isabel upset you. Losing my wife was hard enough. I can't imagine how hard it would be to have lost Isabel, how difficult it must be for you and the Harrisons."

Pain shot through her chest, and she murmured, "It's been hell."

He pulled one hand out of his pocket and flipped it up in a gesture that said she'd proved his point. "And I don't want to make it worse."

She nodded, swallowing hard to force down the knot of emotion that had worked its way up her throat. "I appreciate that. But how selfish would it be of me to expect you not to say what you needed to about your daughter, if it helped you work through your own grief for your wife?"

He lifted his chin and cocked his head as if her comment caught him off guard.

Before he could say anything, she raised a hand. "Besides, I get a little tired of people avoiding mention of babies, and especially Gracie, my daughter, as if pretending she never existed would be easier for me, when really it's their own awkwardness they want to avoid."

She heard the bitter edge in her tone and bit the inside of her cheek. She hadn't meant to snap at him. Her frustrations with her coworkers and neighbors weren't his fault. But instead of taking offense, he smiled and nodded.

"Exactly. I get the same thing from my friends concerning my wife. As if any talk of spouses is suddenly taboo. I hate it."

His response surprised her. Something warm unfurled in her chest, releasing a bit of the pressure that squeezed her lungs. When was the last time someone had actually understood the tangled emotions she had over losing Grace? Even this tiny connection to Jared made her feel a little less alone. "Your wife must have died recently if Isabel is only a year old."

He nodded. "Nine months ago. Isabel was five months old when Kelly was killed by a drunk driver."

A spark of outrage fired through her. "A drunk driver. It's bad enough to lose someone to disease or an accident, but when another person's carelessness is to blame… that's—" She shook her head, fumbling for the right word to voice her dismay.

"Yeah. It is." He gave her a bittersweet smile, telling her he understood what went unsaid.

Empathy pricked her heart, and she felt another thread of connection form between them. His grief might be different, but they faced similar struggles.

"I'm sorry," she muttered, knowing how trite the words sounded. How many people had told her they were sorry for her loss? Enough that the platitude felt empty to her. Judging by his expression, he'd heard a lot of hollow phrases in the past nine months, as well. Well-meant words that did nothing to ease the ache in his heart.

Elise groaned and raised a hand to her face. "Ugh, did I just say that? Not that I'm not sorry about your loss, but—"

He chuckled softly and gave her an understanding look. "I'm sorry for your loss, too. There. Now we're even on banal expressions." He shrugged. "Although I've decided to cut folks a break. I don't think I'd know what to say to any of my friends if their wives died, either. Other than, *Man, that sucks.*"

They shared a wry grin. The flicker of humor in his dark eyes mesmerized her, and after a moment, she realized she was staring at him. He had the kind of face that held a woman's attention—square jaw, full lips, straight nose. As she shook herself from her trance, her pulse fluttered.

She adjusted the strap of her purse on her shoulder and sidled toward the door. "I should be going."

"Right. Well—" He offered his hand. "—It was nice to meet you, Elise."

"You, too." She took his hand, and his long fingers and warm palm folded around hers in an encompassing grasp. Firm. Strong. *Dependable.*

She let her hand linger in his, puzzling over the words that had sprung to mind. Thinking she could tell anything about his character from his handshake was preposterous. And of all the traits a man could be, why was his dependability what came to mind?

"Will you come back next week?"

His question roused her from her sidetracked thoughts. Would she be back? Coming tonight had taken her weeks of preparation and building her nerve. "Maybe. I, um…"

He squeezed her hand before releasing it. "Maybe is good enough. No pressure. Just think about it."

And think, she did. All week. But not just about whether she'd return to the grief-support meeting. She thought about Jared Coleman. The way he'd lost his wife. His one-year-old daughter, who was walking. His dark, compassionate eyes.

When she weighed whether she wanted to return to the support group, her reluctance to open herself to the pain of rehashing Grace's death was tempered by a desire to see Jared again. The connection she'd felt with him had been real. Hadn't it? But was her interest in Jared about feeling less alone in her grief or about the flutter of attraction she'd experienced when he'd held her hand? She wasn't looking for a boyfriend, especially not one with his own baggage and a daughter who'd remind her every day of Gracie. So why did his lopsided smile keep drifting through her mind?

"Goodbye, Princess." Jared kissed his daughter on the top of her head as he moved toward the door the next Thursday night. "Be good for Grandma."

"She's always good. Aren't you, Isabel?" his mother asked as she helped guide Isabel's spoon to her mouth. Which was progress. "Will you be late?"

"Shouldn't be. The support group never runs later than eight o'clock. You know that." He shoved his arms in his jacket, then fumbled in his pocket for his keys.

"What I know is that you don't have any sort of social life," his mother said, and Jared groaned.

Here we go again...

"A handsome young man like you should be dating. It's been almost a year since Kelly died, and—"

"It's been nine months," he corrected, "and I'm not ready to date again. I may never be. No one can ever replace Kelly." He jangled the keys in his hand impatiently. How many times in the past few weeks had he had this same conversation?

"I'm not suggesting anyone replace her. But there are plenty of other women who have merits of their own. There's a perfectly lovely girl in my office who—"

He huffed a sigh of exasperation. "I can find my own dates, Mom."

"But you don't." She aimed Isabel's spoon at him to punctuate her point.

"Because I don't want to date. I told you it's too soon."

"A young man like you has…needs. Physical needs that—"

Jared shuddered. "Stop!" He held up a hand and marched quickly to the back door. "Do *not* go there."

He was *not* discussing his sex life with his mother.

"I'm just saying—"

"See you a little after eight, Mom. Good night!" He exited quickly and shook his head as he strolled to his car. He knew his mother meant well, but the idea of dating again stirred a sharp ache in his chest and an uneasy sense of guilt in his gut. Damn, but he missed Kelly so much some days he could barely stand it.

As he cranked his car's engine, he recalled the new woman who'd visited the grief-support group last week. Elise Norris. Her glossy blonde hair, bright blue eyes and sad smile had filtered through his thoughts at odd moments this past week. While he showered. While he tried to fall asleep. When he woke in the morning.

His pulse kicked up at the prospect of seeing her again tonight, and he frowned to himself. He'd just finished telling his mother that he wasn't ready to date. So why was he anticipating seeing Elise tonight with schoolboylike nerves?

Okay, yes, they'd had a certain connection in the few moments they'd talked, but that was hardly reason to get all worked up. On the heels of the anxious flutter, cumbersome thoughts of Kelly rose to quash any notion of pursuing his attention to Elise. Just five years ago he'd stood at the altar and promised to forsake all others for Kelly.

How could he think of another woman when Kelly hadn't even been gone for a year?

Raising his daughter had to be his focus now. Not finding a new wife.

Elise had almost made up her mind to skip the next support-group meeting when she remembered the Harrisons. Knowing that they'd also lost a baby made her want to reach out to them. If anyone could understand the hole in her heart, she guessed the young couple could. And maybe she could offer them some support, as well.

By the time she arrived at the meeting, there were only two chairs left vacant in the circle. As Joleen called a greeting to her, Elise headed for the chair closest to her, but before she reached it, one of the older ladies, who'd been getting a cup of coffee, took the seat. Which left one open chair. Next to Jared. She met his gaze as she approached the chair, and he flashed her the lopsided smile that had filled her thoughts throughout the week. Her stomach flip-flopped.

"Welcome back," he whispered to her as she settled next to him.

The sandalwood scent she remembered from last week filled her nose and stirred a warmth in her chest.

Joleen called the meeting to order and opened the floor to comments and discussion. Throughout the session, Elise tried to focus on what the other members were saying, tried to work up the nerve to share something that might be valuable to the conversation, but she found herself preoccupied with every movement, every sound Jared made. A grunt of sympathy for Mrs. Bagwell. A scratch of his chin. Crossing his arms over his chest. A heavy breath… of fatigue? Boredom?

When he shifted in his chair and her pulse scrambled,

she castigated herself mentally for her schoolgirl reaction to him. She couldn't remember ever being so hyperaware of a man in her life. What was wrong with her? She'd come to the support group for help managing her grief, not to find a boyfriend!

Elise balled her hands in frustration and made a concerted effort to pay attention to what Kim Harrison was saying. The death of this woman's baby was the primary reason she'd returned to the support group.

"...like Jared said last week. I think a lot about the could-have-beens. What her laugh would have sounded like, what her favorite food would have been, whether she'd have been good at sports." Kim looked over at Elise then. "Do you ever do that? Think about what your baby might have done, who she'd have been?"

Elise's breath snagged. "I...yeah. A lot. Almost constantly. When I'm not wondering what went wrong, what I could have done differently during my pregnancy that might have saved her, why this happened to me when she was my one shot at being a mother."

Mrs. Bagwell frowned. "Why do you think you won't have other children? You're still young."

Elise gripped the edge of her seat, startled by the older woman's question. Taking a breath for composure, she studied the woman's face and saw nothing but concern and confusion, not judgment. "Well, the procedure I used to get pregnant with Grace took most of my savings. Since I'm unmarried, not in a relationship and not into one-night stands, the chances of getting pregnant the natural way are pretty nonexistent."

Mrs. Bagwell seemed unfazed by her bluntness. "I see. I've learned, though, never to underestimate the surprises and twists of fate life can hold. Why, by this time next year, you could be happily wed and expecting again." The older woman punctuated her comment with a satisfied nod and sat back in her chair with a confident smile.

Elise could only gape, speechless.

"I suppose that's true," Joleen said. "Holding on to optimism is always a good thing, but let's look at some ways Elise can deal with the issues she's facing now. Kim, how do you handle those could-have-been thoughts when you have them?"

Kim glanced at her husband. "I talk about them with Greg. And here, with all of you. That helps. Sometimes I post my feelings to the online message board I've mentioned before." Kim directed her attention to Elise. "I'll give you the link. It's another support group I found. A message board for parents who've lost children whether to death or kidnapping or divorce. There's lots of information and links to great resources. You should look into it."

Elise nodded to Kim. "Thanks. I will."

The meeting continued, with the discussion turning to Mrs. Fenwick's late husband, before the group adjourned promptly at the end of the hour. As promised, Kim caught up to Elise by the refreshment table and handed her a scrap of paper with a URL printed neatly in pink ink.

"Here's the address for the message board. I know an online group seems impersonal, but the people are really helpful and sometimes it is easier to be honest about your feelings when you're not face-to-face with the people you're sharing with. You can be as anonymous or open with your identity as you want. I hope you'll try it."

Elise tucked the paper in her pocket. "Thanks. I'll check it out." She smiled her appreciation. This exchange of information, this opportunity to get to know the Harrisons, was exactly the reason she'd come tonight. Seizing the chance to speak privately with Kim, Elise cleared her throat and asked, "So…if you don't mind my asking…how did your daughter die?"

"I don't mind. In fact, I wanted to talk to you about it. Because of how your daughter died and all…" Kim said, leaning toward Elise and placing a hand on her arm.

Elise shook her head. "What does Grace's death have to do with your baby?"

Kim shrugged. "Maybe nothing. But I thought it was an odd coincidence is all."

"Coincidence?"

"Yeah." Kim's face darkened. "Our little girl died at the hospital, too. Just hours after she was born."

Chapter 2

Elise heard a buzzing in her ears, and her head swam. When her knees buckled, she groped futilely for something to brace against. As she stumbled back a step, she encountered the warm, solid wall of a chest, and a strong hand grasped her elbow, steadying her. The scent of sandalwood surrounded her, piercing her fog of shock. And she knew without looking who supported her.

"Elise?" Jared's deep voice rumbled near her ear.

"I'm sorry." Kim rushed forward, concern knitting her brow. "Maybe I shouldn't have said anything. I didn't mean to—"

"No. I…I'm okay. I was just…caught off guard. Everything about losing Grace just flooded back and—" She swallowed hard and blinked at Kim as the truth the woman had shared sank in. "Your baby died at the hospital, too? I…Was she premature?"

Kim shook her head. "Right on time. To the day. But

she apparently had a heart defect that our doctor missed during my pregnancy."

An eerie prickle nipped her neck. "Her heart stopped, and they couldn't resuscitate her," she whispered raggedly.

Kim blinked. "Yes. How did you—?" Her eyes widened. "You mean Grace—?"

Elise's voice stuck in her throat. The only sound she could make came out as a moan.

Behind her, Jared muttered a curse. "That sounds too suspicious to be a coincidence. The odds…"

"What hospital did you use?" Kim asked.

Elise struggled for her composure, sucking in a calming breath. "My labor started while I was out of town at a crafts fair. I went to a little hospital in Pine Mill…."

Kim frowned and shook her head. "No. We were at Crestview General."

Something like disappointment punctured the breath Elise had been holding. As tragic and macabre as the similarities in their losses were, hope had flickered briefly that she was on to some answers regarding Grace's mysterious death.

"So many times I've wondered if our baby would have made it if we'd been here in Lagniappe at St. Mary's where they have the PICU," Kim said.

"What-ifs are natural," Jared said quietly, "but you can make yourself crazy with them. Don't torture yourself, Kim."

She lifted a corner of her mouth in acknowledgment. "Easier said than done."

"Ready to go?" Greg asked, stepping up behind his wife.

"Sure." Kim turned back to Elise. "See you next time?"

Elise nodded and, still rather numb with shock, searched for her voice. "I—yeah. Bye."

As the Harrisons departed, Jared stepped around to

face Elise and dipped his head to get a better look at her expression. "Are you okay?"

Elise raked her blond hair back with her fingers. "I don't know," she answered honestly. "I really don't know what to make of this."

"It is pretty hard to believe. I mean, if this were 1811, maybe. But with modern health and medicine what it is, you'd think…" He stopped himself and shoved his hands in his pockets. "Well…anyway."

"The doctors should have been able to save her. That's what you were going to say, wasn't it?" Elise asked, meeting his gaze. Last week, she'd thought they'd reached an unspoken agreement to be candid with each other. His honesty about his grief had been at the heart of the connection she'd felt with him.

He furrowed his brow with a guilty look. "Yeah. Something like that."

She sighed. "Tiptoeing around delicate topics is so tedious. Can we agree not to play that game? We both know it serves no purpose."

He gave her a nod and a relieved smile. "Agreed."

"In that case, yes. I've got plenty of questions about why the doctors and modern medicine didn't save Grace. And now, in light of what Kim said about their baby dying the same way…" Elise lifted a trembling hand, flipping her palm up in frustration. "What am I supposed to make of that?"

Jared didn't answer. Instead, he glanced toward the kitchen area where Joleen was cleaning up the last of the refreshments. "Would you like to go somewhere? Get a cup of coffee?"

"I— Don't you need to get home? I'm sure babysitters are expensive."

"They can be. But my mom watches Isabel when I come

here." He paused and jingled the keys in his pocket. "I know Kim just dropped a bomb on you, and I don't want you going home alone to stew and drive yourself crazy over the news."

Elise lifted a corner of her mouth. "That's what I'd do. You're right."

"I'd be happy to be your sounding board for a while."

When was the last time someone had offered to just listen to her, let her vent and unburden her heart? Too long. Gratitude for his thoughtfulness tugged in her chest.

"I'd like that. How about Brewer's Café? It's just a couple blocks from here."

He gave a nod and a smile. "Meet you there in five."

Jared climbed behind his steering wheel and blew out a long, cleansing breath. What the hell was he doing? Hadn't he just told his mother tonight that he wasn't ready to date?

"Okay, so this is not a date. *Not,*" he muttered to himself as he gripped the steering wheel and stared out the windshield into the church parking lot. Despite his denials, guilt thumped a drumbeat in his chest. "You're just giving your support to another group member who had a shock tonight. It's not a date."

So why were his palms damp with sweat, and why was his conscience pricking him with images of Kelly in the last days they spent together?

Not a date. Not a date… He let the words repeat in his brain as he backed his car out of the parking space and pulled up behind Elise to follow her to Brewer's Café.

He recalled the look in Elise's eyes when she'd learned how the Harrisons' baby had died, and sympathy twisted inside him. No matter how conflicted he felt about meeting Elise for coffee, he wanted to be there for her tonight.

Elise was in shock and needed a friend. He could be her friend without it meaning anything else, couldn't he?

Of course. He released a deep breath. It was not a date.

"Tell me about Isabel," Elise said after twenty minutes of small talk. She cradled her mug of cappuccino, which had grown cold, and met his startled look with an encouraging nod.

"Are you sure? Doesn't hearing other people talk about their kids hurt?"

She sighed. "Of course it does. But am I supposed to avoid people with kids the rest of my life?"

He took a slow deep breath. "No."

"Do you have a picture of her?"

He chuckled, reaching into his back pocket for his wallet. "Seriously? You have to ask?"

She returned his grin. "A long shot, I know, but…"

He flipped open the wallet and turned it so she could see the bright-eyed cherub with blond curls. Elise's breath caught, and it took a moment to recover. Like all babies, Isabel was precious, but something about her sweet smile and chubby cheeks grabbed Elise by the throat.

"Wow," she rasped when she found enough air to talk. "Look at those curls. Believe it or not, I had curls like that when I was younger." She tugged on her straight hair and scoffed. "I'd kill for a few natural curls now."

"Those curls make for a pretty wild-looking bedhead after her naps, let me tell you," he said with a soft laugh. He flipped the picture to show her another more recent shot of his daughter. Two teeth peeked from her happy grin, and she wore a lacy white dress with a matching bow in her golden-colored hair. "This was at her baptism a couple months ago."

Elise admired the shot, fighting down the bittersweet

pang clambering inside her. Opposite the picture of Isabel was a picture of a raven-haired woman with olive skin and large almond-shaped eyes. Elise pointed to the woman. "Kelly?"

He nodded.

"She was beautiful."

"Thanks. I think so, too."

Elise bit her bottom lip in thought and studied the picture of Isabel again. "I'm trying to decide which of you Isabel favors more, but…"

"But…you don't see any resemblance to either of us. Am I right?"

"Well…"

"That's because she was adopted. Kelly couldn't have children."

Elise's gaze darted to Jared's. "Oh…I—" She didn't know how to respond, so she changed the subject. "So your family lives in town and helps you take care of Isabel. That's pretty handy."

"Yeah, most of my family is local." He closed the wallet and put it back in his pocket. "My mom and dad live across town, and I have a brother and sister-in-law, Michelle, who live just a couple blocks away. My sister-in-law is the one who keeps her while I'm at work." He tipped his head in inquiry. "What about you? Any family?"

"A brother who deigns to talk to his younger sister when I call him."

Jared arched an eyebrow. "He has something against talking to family?"

"Naw. He's just busy and doesn't think about calling his little sister. We're not especially close. After our mother died, our dad couldn't be bothered with raising kids, and we ended up in foster homes. Sometimes together, more often, not. I think he put an emotional distance between us as a defense mechanism. It hurts less to be separated from someone you only care marginally about."

Jared was quiet for a moment, studying her. "But clearly family is important to you. You make the effort to stay in touch with your brother."

She sighed and stared at the tabletop, idly tracing a crack in the top with her finger. "Yeah. And I was planning to raise a child alone, planning to start my family even if there was no husband in the picture." Jared didn't comment right away, and she glanced up when she sensed his reluctance to say what was on his mind. "Go ahead…ask. Remember, we promised to be candid with each other."

He flashed her a lopsided grin. "Right. I was just wondering why you never married."

"I actually thought I'd found Mr. Right a few years ago, but it turns out I was too late. His wife found him first."

He gave her an appropriately sympathetic groan.

"After that humiliation, I swore off dating for a while." She pulled a grimace then took a sip of cold cappuccino.

He grunted and cocked his head. "A loss to all single men. Any guy would be lucky to have a date with a lovely lady like you. I hate it when the jerks go and ruin things for the rest of us honest guys."

The comment may have been the standard polite response, but it still caught Elise off guard. She yanked her gaze up to him, and the warmth of his smile stirred a flickering pulse inside her.

"I—I wasn't fishing for a compliment." She chuckled awkwardly. "Really. I—"

Their waitress arrived just in time to save her from her fumbling. After refilling Jared's mug, their server left their check and bustled back to the counter.

"So…you want to talk about the elephant in the room

now? The reason I asked you here before you went home?" he asked.

Elise's gut tightened. "It's a lot to process. Accepting that Grace died of a freak heart condition hours after birth was hard enough. But to think the same type of thing happened to another couple in town within months of Grace's death is…spooky. Unsettling."

"Exactly." He furrowed his brow. "Did the doctor give you a medical explanation for Grace's death? Was an autopsy done?"

"Yes. As I understand it, there was. All they told me was she had a weak heart, and she died of heart failure. I know I should have asked more questions, but to be honest, I was kinda numb."

"I can understand that. I remember the shock that put me in a sort of daze after Kelly died. I got through it because my family rallied around me to help."

She gave him a wan smile. "You're lucky to have them."

"Yeah, I am." He gave her a nod and a smile that said he was counting his blessings. She didn't want to envy Jared for the support he had from his family, but the ache of loneliness she'd carried in her bones since losing Grace swamped her with a dizzying wallop.

Clearing her throat, she forged on, not wanting him to see how vulnerable and alone she felt. "So I've been thinking about asking the hospital for Gracie's medical file, but I've been putting it off because…well, I knew it would be hard. I'm kinda torn between wanting to know all the details to find some answers and shutting it all in the past and trying to move on."

He nodded, his gaze focused on her, letting her know he was listening. She knew he didn't have magic answers, but having him as a sounding board helped more than she'd expected. After months of carrying so much turmoil inside, having someone to listen to her ramble and unburden herself felt incredibly good, freeing.

"I mean, I know that, being a small hospital, they didn't have the neonatal ICU facilities that might have saved her. Like Kim was saying tonight about the lack of advanced care at Crestview General, I've wondered so often what would have happened if I'd not been out of town that day I went into labor."

He rolled one palm up. "Maybe that's all it is. Maybe babies die at smaller hospitals more frequently because of the limited facilities. I mean, years ago, women and babies died during childbirth pretty regularly."

She bit her bottom lip, considering his point. "Maybe."

"If I were you…" he started and waited for her to meet his gaze as if seeking permission to be so bold as to give unsolicited advice.

She locked onto the incisive spark in his eyes, hungry for whatever guidance he had. "Yeah?"

"I'd make some inquiries. See if there are reports of other cases similar to yours at that hospital. Compare what you learn to the mortality rate of bigger hospitals. Gather facts, look for a pattern, see what comes out in the wash."

"You don't think Grace's case was an isolated incident?" She narrowed an intent gaze on him. "You basically said as much earlier tonight…that Kim's loss was too similar to be a coincidence."

He spread his hands. "I don't know. I may have been talking out of turn. But yeah, my initial gut instinct said something fishy was going on."

Her heart beat an anxious tattoo. "Fishy as in…?"

He waved her off. "I don't want to speculate. Look, Kim mentioned an online community with a message board. That's a good place to start. Arm yourself with information."

"That I can do. Between the internet and my contacts through the newspaper, I think I can get plenty of information."

He arched one eyebrow. "You work at the paper?"

"Staff photographer," she said, turning the conversation to her job. Next, he told her about his position as foreman with a local, family-owned construction company. As they swapped stories about their work, education and acquaintances they had in common, the mood between them relaxed and fell into the time-honored patterns of a first date. Elise found Jared easy to talk to, and she experienced a tingling rush in her blood whenever he flashed his lopsided grin.

"Well, it worked," she said almost an hour later when she checked her watch. "Your pleasant company has kept my mind off what Kim told me tonight and saved me from sitting alone at home agonizing over what it could mean."

He gave her a satisfied smile. "Mission accomplished."

"I hope I haven't kept you too late."

He shrugged. "My mother might be a bit worried about what kept me, but as soon as she hears I was having coffee with an attractive lady, all will be forgiven. She's been encouraging me to start dating again."

A knot of regret tightened in Elise's chest. "Jared, I, uh…I'm not in a place where I…well, I'm not ready to date. I'm not looking for a relationship."

He nodded and raised a hand. "That's fine. I'm not sure I'm ready to date again, either. But…" He twisted his mouth in a thoughtful moue, and his eyes took on a devilish spark. "We don't have to tell my mother. As long as she thinks we might be an item, maybe she'll back off trying to fix me up with her single friends."

Elise scrunched her nose in a sympathetic wince and chuckled. "Oh, no."

"Oh, yes." A low, melodic laugh rumbled from his chest. "And let's just say, there is a reason some of her friends are still single." He rolled his eyes and whistled. "So the true nature of our friendship can be our little secret. Deal?"

She laughed harder, savoring the feeling. How long had it been since she had a reason to laugh? "So you want me to be your fake girlfriend?"

He pulled a face. "Well, we might not have to take it that far, but I'd consider it a personal favor if you'd be my excuse for not meeting Linda-from-accounting or Betty-from-her-scrapbooking-club."

She flashed him a sassy grin. "Yeah, and what do I get out of this deal?"

He leaned back in the booth and folded his arms over his chest. "An occasional cup of coffee, maybe dinner or a movie once or twice." He winked, and his cheek tugged up in a playful grin. "And, of course, my charming company and scintillating conversation."

"Gosh, I don't know…" She rubbed her chin and pursed her lips as if struggling with the decision, as if agreeing would be a hardship.

In truth, the hardest part of such an agreement would be *not* developing any romantic feelings for Jared. He was handsome, kind, thoughtful and funny. Exactly the kind of man she could fall for—if she were looking for a boyfriend. But, as alone as she felt most of the time, involvement with a man who had a one-year-old daughter would be…torture. Anguish. She was bound to form attachments to Isabel, painful reminders of what she'd lost, bonds that would add to her grief when they were inevitably broken. Because Jared wasn't looking for a new wife. He clearly still loved his late wife. Elise had already made the mistake of falling for a married man, and she wanted no part of a love triangle—even if the third party was a ghost.

"Wow," Jared said with a self-deprecating scoff when she hesitated a moment too long, "I didn't realize being my decoy was such an onerous favor to ask."

"Oh!" With a startled laugh, she shook herself from her thoughts and reached across the table to grasp his arm. "Oh, no… I was just thinking. I'd love to have coffee with you again. It's better than sitting home by myself stewing over tragedies."

He gave her a comically pained expression. "Ouch. Maybe I should quit while I'm behind."

She slapped a hand over her mouth, laughing softly. "That didn't come out right. I didn't mean…"

Shaking his head, he grinned and slid to the end of the booth, picking up the check as he stood. "Just say goodnight, Gracie."

Gracie.

Though she knew he was quoting George Burns from his old radio show with his wife, Elise felt the blood drain from her face, and her heartbeat slowed. Jeez, she was a mess, if just the mention of her daughter's name still delivered an instant breath-stealing jolt.

Jared's face fell, and he dropped back on the booth bench, reaching for her. "Cripes, I'm sorry. That was thoughtless of—"

She covered his mouth with her fingers, and his warm breath tickled her palm. "Don't apologize. Remember—no tiptoeing around each other."

He wrapped his hand around her wrist and pressed a kiss on her palm. "Right."

The scratch of his five o'clock shadow on her skin sent a ripple of sweet sensation to her core. Inhaling deeply to steady herself, she mustered a smile for him and said softly, "Good night, Gracie."

* * *

Jared stayed in her thoughts as she drove home, and she caught herself smiling when she remembered his hand-kiss, his teasing, his dark bedroom eyes. Jared had been a pleasant distraction tonight, but as she parked in her driveway, her conversation with Kim replayed in her mind.

Two babies. Two hospitals. Two stopped hearts.

And Jared's muttered curse. *That sounds too suspicious to be a coincidence.*

The similarities in Grace's and the Harrisons' baby's deaths rankled, but what did she really know? She was no doctor. Maybe the sudden death of infants was more common than she knew. She'd heard of SIDS, Sudden Infant Death Syndrome, when babies died mysteriously in their sleep. Maybe Grace's death was related to that?

Information. As Jared suggested, she needed to gather some facts before she drew any conclusions that would serve no purpose other than making her paranoid.

She bustled into her house, a chill autumn wind following her inside. Her black-and-brown tabby, Brooke, greeted her and trotted into the kitchen, winding around Elise's legs as she begged for her supper.

"Hey, Brookie Wookie. Hang on. Dinner's coming." She fixed herself a cup of chamomile tea, poured Brooke a bowl of food, then set up her laptop. Placing her mug beside her computer, Elise typed *infant mortality rates* in an internet search engine. Within a few key strokes, Elise had learned that Louisiana's infant mortality rate of ten deaths per thousand births was higher than the national average. She also found breakdowns of infant deaths by race and region. The statistics, while eye-opening, didn't provide her the detailed information she wanted.

She rocked back in her chair, and Brooke took the opportunity to hop into her lap. She idly scratched Brooke's head and twisted her mouth in thought. Wouldn't a hospital's records be a matter of public information? Data on all births and deaths at a hospital would have to be reported to the government, wouldn't it? If she could get her hands on the records of Pine Mill Hospital, she could compare the information to the state and national average.

Reaching awkwardly around Brooke to type, she tried a more specific search for Pine Mill Hospital's yearly data, birth and infant-death totals, but hit a dead end. However the search terms *infant death* and *Pine Mill* led her to a two-year-old obituary in the *Pine Mill Gazette* for the infant son of a local couple.

Elise scanned the article with her heart in her throat. The baby had died of unknown causes just after his birth at Pine Mill Hospital. Her hand shaking, she hit Print to add the article to her file.

That made three infant deaths from mysterious causes within a matter of months, all in a small geographic region. Three that she knew of. How many more otherwise healthy babies had died tragically within hours of their births?

Did she dare contact the parents of the baby boy mentioned in the two-year-old obituary for more information? They could have heard of similar cases, just as she was learning of stories similar to Grace's. She didn't want to stir up painful memories for them without good cause.

As Jared suggested, perhaps her best move for now was to solicit information regarding similar cases. Remembering the online community message board Kim had mentioned at the grief-support meeting, Elise lifted Brooke off her lap and dug the scrap of paper with the URL out of her pocket. When she reached the home page, she created an account for herself and logged on.

On the first screen, she found a list of the most recent posts and replies. As Kim had said, the topics varied from posts about missing children, questions about legal rights and suggestions for surviving the holidays without your loved one.

She spent several minutes reading the various discussion threads and found the replies of the members to be both helpful and compassionate. No wonder Kim recommended the website. Elise sipped her tea and began mentally composing her introduction. Should she make an official request for information or simply explain what happened to her and see if it solicited replies of similar incidents?

After some thought, she chose to keep her first foray on the message board simple and see what came of it. She could always request similar stories later. At the end of her post, she gave a secondary email address she used for online shopping as her contact info. Taking a deep breath, she clicked the submit button, and her post vanished into the vast beyond. A few seconds later it appeared on the message board.

"Well, Brooke," she said, stroking the cat's back as the tabby rubbed against her leg. "All I can do now is wait and see who replies."

Jared tiptoed into Isabel's nursery and peered over the edge of her crib to check on his daughter before heading to bed himself. He could stand there for hours and never get tired of watching his little angel sleep. But as usual, the tenderness of the moment, Isabel's innocence and late hour were a potent brew that brought a pang of grief for what Kelly was missing. And for how much he missed Kelly.

Tonight, however, his memories of Kelly were tinged with a shade of guilt. He knew the source.

Elise.

He'd had a good time with Elise, had felt comfortable talking with her, had felt natural teasing her. And had been attracted to her. Powerfully so.

Maybe that was the root of his guilt. He'd had female friends while Kelly was alive, but his attraction to Elise seemed a bit like a betrayal of Kelly's memory. He knew he was being ridiculous. Moving on, dating again, didn't mean he loved Kelly any less or that he'd forgotten her. If the situation was reversed, he'd want Kelly to have a second chance for love and companionship. A life partner to help her raise Isabel. In his heart, he knew Kelly would say the same for him. But his attraction to Elise still left him off-balance somehow. He wasn't ready to start a new relationship....

Was he?

He brushed a wayward curl away from Isabel's cheek, and a pang tugged his heart. Maybe he was unsettled being around Elise because he knew how blessed he was to have Isabel, while Elise had lost her best chance to be a parent, had been stripped of the treasure he savored every day.

He shuddered when he thought about losing Isabel. One of the reasons he and Kelly had chosen the private agency they used to adopt Isabel had been the agency's assurances that the closed adoption process they employed meant the birth parents had forfeited all claims to Isabel. Their greatest fear had been to have one of the birth parents change their mind and try to take Isabel from them after the adoption closed. Just considering that scenario lit a fiery determination in his belly. He'd fight anyone who tried to take Isabel from him with every resource possible. Isabel was *his*.

Chapter 3

"Elise, I want you to go with Russell when he covers the ribbon cutting at the new monkey house at the zoo today."

Elise hurriedly minimized the website she'd been reading and spun in her chair to face her boss. The newspaper had rather lax rules about using the office computers for personal business, but she'd been checking for replies to her post on the Parents Without Children forum and wanted to protect her privacy.

"Be sure to get lots of shots of the mayor and town council members, not just the animals." The editor-in-chief put a sticky note on her desk with "zoo ribbon cutting—2:00 p.m." scrawled across it.

She moved the sticky note to her date book. "Yes, sir. Uh, Mr. Grimes?" she called before he could disappear back into his office. He turned and waited for her to speak.

She cleared her throat. "I'd like to do some kind of

special piece, maybe for a weekend edition, with a photo spread and feature article—"

"About the monkey house?" He frowned and propped his hands on his ample hips.

"Oh…no. No. About the people in the region. Small business owners. Veterans with interesting stories from the war. Maybe someone with an unusual hobby. Something with local color." *Something that might give me a better platform for my work than ribbon cuttings at monkey houses.* "I'd write the accompanying article myself."

"You can write?"

"I think I write pretty well."

He arched an eyebrow and grunted. "Since you used *well* correctly, instead of saying you write *good*—a pet peeve of mine—I'd be willing to consider it. No promises." He rubbed a hand across his mouth and chin as he thought. "Get me a specific idea and sample copy, and we'll talk."

"I will. Thank you." She smiled to herself as she turned back to her computer. As much as she loved photography, she knew the newspaper was struggling. Too many people had started getting their news online or from television. Rumors of staff cuts had been circulating, and she wanted to showcase her other talents and prove herself useful to the higher-ups. And she aspired to doing more with her photojournalism than snapping shots of the mayor glad-handing at ribbon cuttings.

A face appeared over the partition between cubicles. "Are you trying to put me out of a job?"

She glanced up at Russell Prine, the features editor, and shook her head. "No one could replace you, Russell. Why, I'd be surprised if your piece on the garden club's bazaar doesn't win a Pulitzer."

She flashed a teasing grin, and he rolled his eyes. "Very

funny. So, Miss Snark, want to ride with me to the big
zoo shindig?"

"Sure. Thanks."

"I'm leaving in an hour." Russell disappeared again
behind the cubicle wall, and Elise opened the web page
for the forum again.

She had her first three replies. Holding her breath, she
opened the first one.

Elise arrived at the grief-support meeting early the next
week. She was eager to tell Jared what she'd learned so
far, and, if she was honest, she had been looking forward
to spending more time with the charming widower. She
scanned the room but saw no sign of him. Yet.

Having skipped dinner, she swiped a couple of cookies from the refreshment table before she took a seat in
the circle, carefully choosing one that had an open chair
next to it where Jared could sit. She nibbled a cookie and
watched the door for him to arrive.

*Good heavens, you're acting like a scheming teenager
with a crush.* She gave her head a shake. For someone who
wasn't interested in a relationship, she'd certainly spent a
lot of time anticipating the meeting tonight and thinking
about Jared Coleman.

"—Are you tonight?"

Elise snapped out of her daze when she realized Mr.
Miller was speaking to her. "Oh, I'm sorry. What did you
say?"

The older gentleman grinned. "I asked how you were
doing, but since you were smiling, I'll assume you're doing
well."

She'd been smiling? "Oh, yes. I'm doing pretty well.
And you?"

Mr. Miller used her rhetorical inquiry as an excuse to

regale her with his medical history with an emphasis on his current arthritis issues. Elise patiently listened, trying to act interested in what the man was telling her about his knee-replacement surgery, while sending furtive glances toward the door.

When Jared appeared, a small sigh of relief escaped from her before she saw what was in his arms and she caught her breath again. *Isabel.*

He had a large diaper bag over one shoulder, and his golden-haired daughter perched on his hip as he talked to Joleen. Mr. Miller's monologue faded to a drone as Elise stared, her heart in her throat. She'd been eager to see Jared again but totally unprepared for seeing his daughter. Who was the age Grace would have been. Who had her thumb in her mouth and her head tucked shyly on Jared's shoulder. Jared gestured to Isabel then to the door.

Elise bit her bottom lip. Was he leaving? Had something happened?

Joleen shook her head and waved him toward the chairs with a smile then tickled Isabel's leg. Jared nodded and started toward the circle, his gaze latching instantly on Elise's. The smile that lit his face as he approached fueled a giddy kick in her pulse.

Oh, Elise, you are in trouble.

"Hi," he said. "Anyone sitting there?" He hitched his head toward the chair beside her.

"You." She reached for the diaper bag and helped him get settled. "No babysitter tonight?"

The older ladies sitting nearby cooed and grinned at Isabel as he took his seat.

"Michelle has the stomach flu, and my parents had plans. If my having Isabel here makes you uncomfortable, I don't have to stay."

Her heart squeezed as she caught a whiff of baby powder

mixed with Jared's sandalwood. If she needed a reminder of why falling for Jared was a bad idea, the sharp-edged longing that knifed through her gut as she inhaled Isabel's sweet scent sent a clear message. She wasn't ready to be around Jared's daughter, a too-poignant reminder of her loss.

But Elise cleared the knot of emotion that stuck in her throat and shook her head. "No, don't go. She's fine. I—"

"Kee," a tiny voice said, halting Elise mid-thought.

She dropped her gaze to Isabel, who stared at her with wide blue eyes and pointed a chubby finger at Elise's lap.

"What?" Elise glanced to Jared for help interpreting.

"She sees your cookies." He shot her a lopsided grin. "What can I say? My girl's got a sweet tooth."

"Kee!" Isabel said louder, eliciting another round of adoring sighs and grins from the older ladies.

"May she have one?" Elise asked, picking one of the sugar cookies off her plate.

"I suppose. She had a pretty good supper."

Her pulse pounding, Elise extended the cookie to Isabel, and the toddler's eyes lit with delight. She gave Elise a shy, four-toothed grin as she accepted her offering.

"Shall we begin?" Joleen said, calling the meeting to order.

Though she was well-behaved, Isabel proved a huge distraction for Elise throughout the meeting. First Elise watched, mesmerized, as the little girl gummed the sugar cookie to oblivion. Then, when the first cookie was gone, Isabel sent Elise a wide-eyed look that clearly asked, "More?"

Elise darted a glance to Jared, who seemed engrossed in what Joleen was telling Mr. Miller, and she furtively slipped another cookie to Isabel.

"Kee!" Isabel kicked her feet happily and flopped back against her father's chest to munch her treat.

Jared spotted the new cookie and raised an eyebrow at Elise. She returned a shrug and a guilty grin that won an indulgent smile from Jared.

After finishing her second cookie Isabel grew restless and wiggled free of Jared's lap. He grabbed for the back of her shirt to catch her before she toddled off, but she tottered straight to Elise's knees. When Isabel wobbled, Elise steadied the baby, who then grabbed Elise's pants with a cookie-smeared fist for balance. Her heart somersaulted, and warmth expanded in Elise's chest.

"Sorry," Jared said, reaching for his daughter.

Elise batted his hands away. "She's fine, Dad."

His look said, "Are you sure?"

Nodding, she smoothed a hand over Isabel's curls and met the girl's blinking blue-eyed gaze. The full feeling in her lungs gave a bittersweet twist. Maternal yearning clawed inside her, but she fought down the ache.

When Isabel held her arms up to her, a stab of tenderness and affection pierced her heart. Elise lifted Jared's daughter onto her lap and gave Isabel a friendly smile. Isabel glanced once to her father, as if for reassurance and approval, then leaned into Elise's chest with a shy grin. Spying the napkin that had held the cookies in Elise's hand, Isabel tugged at the corner and craned her neck to look for more treats.

"All gone," Elise murmured.

"Kee?" Innocent baby blues blinked at her.

"Sorry."

Isabel gave a sweet sigh of resignation and stuck her thumb in her mouth as she tucked her head against Elise for the last few minutes of the meeting.

Jared smiled at them as the meeting dismissed. "I think she's made a new friend."

"Bribery works wonders." She stroked Isabel's back and gave Jared a wry look. "The question is, would she have been as trusting of me had I not fed her cookies?"

Jared chuckled and lifted Isabel from Elise's lap. "Oh, I'm sure the cookies were the deciding factor. She's got a real sweet tooth, I'm afraid."

"Ah, a girl after my own heart." She watched Jared shoulder the diaper bag and remembered her eagerness to talk to him about her fact-finding efforts this week. "I did what you suggested about arming myself with information."

Jared glanced up from tugging a sweater onto Isabel's arms. "Oh, yeah? And?"

"I found some interesting things." She sighed. "I'd hoped we could get coffee again and talk about what I discovered, but…"

He glanced from her to Isabel and back to her. "Oh. Sorry. Can't tonight." He paused and drew his dark eyebrows together. "Unless…"

"Yeah?"

"You could follow us back to my place. I brew a pretty decent cup of coffee, and my mother brought over an apple coffee cake this morning."

"Oh, I don't want to impose." Going to a coffee shop for a chat was one thing, but visiting Jared at his house felt…too personal.

"No imposition. The coffee cake is low fat."

To buy herself time to think, Elise flashed a lopsided grin. "Low fat, huh? What are you telling me?"

He squeezed his eyes shut and chuckled. "I did it again, didn't I? I wasn't implying anything, I just—"

"I was kidding," she said with a laugh, compelled to

save him from his embarrassment. Then before she could talk herself out of it, she added, "Yes, I'll come. Thanks."

While Elise held Isabel, Jared keyed open his front door and led his guest inside. Isabel had fallen asleep in the car, and since he'd had the foresight, due to experience, to change her diaper and put her in her pajamas before he left the grief-support meeting, he only needed to slip her carefully into bed and she'd be down for the night. Fingers crossed.

"I'll take her," he whispered. "As soon as I get her in bed, I'll start a pot of coffee for us."

"Or…point me toward her room, and I'll put her down. One less transfer that risks waking her."

He nodded. "Good thinking. Follow me."

Jared showed Elise to Isabel's room and stood by the crib as she gently eased his daughter onto the mattress. Once she had Isabel positioned for safe sleep, Elise stroked his daughter's curls and ran a crooked finger along her plump cheek. "Good night, sweet girl."

Jared studied the poignant expression Elise wore as she gazed at Isabel, and his chest tightened. An all-too-familiar ache and gnawing guilt ate at him. How many nights had he stood here beside Kelly as she put Isabel to bed? How could it feel so wrong to be standing beside his daughter's bed with a different woman, and yet have it still feel so… right?

Elise would have made a terrific mother. Still would someday. He had no doubt that Elise would be given a second chance to have children of her own. Fate simply *couldn't* be so cruel as to deny this loving woman a chance to be a mother after all she'd already suffered.

Elise drew a ragged-sounding breath and made a hasty retreat from the nursery. Concern jabbed him, but before he pursued her, he spread a light blanket over Isabel, turned on the baby monitor beside her crib, and shooed Bubba, who'd been sleeping on the rocking chair, out of the room.

"Come on, Bubba," he said to the sleepy cat, who rubbed against his leg. "Dinner time."

Bubba gave a rather girlish meow and fell in step behind him as he headed down the hall.

He found Elise in the kitchen, filling the coffee carafe with water at the sink.

"You all right?" He stepped up beside her and angled his head to get a better view of her face.

She nodded. "Yeah."

But he heard tears in her voice, and her hand shook as she poured the water into the coffeemaker.

He turned and took the filters and coffee from the cabinet. Handing her a filter, he searched for the right words to comfort her. Knowing he had what she ached for but had lost sliced him with an odd sense of selfishness and guilty gratitude. Was this how survivors of a fatal accident felt about those who lost their lives?

"Elise—"

"It's not what you think." She faced him, and while her eyes were damp, she seemed remarkably composed. "Yes, I'm thinking about all I'm missing with Grace, but I got emotional because—" She sighed "—Isabel just looked so sweet and innocent. Peaceful. It was beautiful. I cry over things like sunsets and Christmas carols, too. I'm just a sentimental and weepy kind of girl. Sorry."

He eyed her through a narrowed gaze, gauging whether to buy her explanation. "Christmas carols, huh?"

"Well, not the upbeat ones, but 'Silent Night' gets me every time. And 'Away In A Manger.'" She held up a hand. "Don't get me started."

"I'll remember that." He stepped closer and wiped the moisture from her bottom eyelashes with his thumb.

She caught her breath, and her lips parted in surprise. He held her startled gaze, sinking into the fathomless blue of her eyes. Eyes like the ocean, deep and full of mystery. She grew still, except for slowly drawing her bottom lip between her teeth.

The action drew his attention to her mouth, and he acknowledged again how beautiful she was. Not in a high-maintenance, movie-star way, but in a softer way that he found far sexier. He wanted to taste the lip she nibbled, kiss away the haunted look that shadowed her gaze and made her appear so…vulnerable. It was that fragility that made him step back and drop his hand. He liked Elise too much to do anything to hurt her or ruin their budding friendship. Giving her his support and understanding as she negotiated the minefield of her grief was what mattered.

He cleared his throat. "Regular or decaf?"

She blinked as if shaking herself from a trance. "Uh, decaf, I guess." She flashed a wry grin. "Not that caffeine is the reason I can't sleep most nights, but why add fuel to the fire?"

"So why have you been losing sleep? What did you find in your research?"

"If you have a computer, I can show you."

"Sure, it's set up in my office. First door on the left." He hitched his head toward the hall. "Help yourself. I'll be in as soon as the coffee's brewing and I've fed the cats."

"You have cats?" She glanced around the floor.

"Why? Are you allergic?"

"No. In fact, I have one myself. I just…didn't picture you as a cat person."

"They were Kelly's when we married. They've grown on me." He put a can on the electric can opener and as soon as the motor whirred, Bubba and Diva trotted in from the next room and began circling his feet. Diva added a few loud meows, begging him to hurry.

Elise chuckled. "Wow, the black one is hungry. Hope she doesn't wake Isabel with that racket."

"Yeah, Diva's got some pipes on her, doesn't she?" He set the bowls of food on the floor, and the cats dived in.

"Diva?"

"Yep. And she lives up to her name. She can be a real prima donna, and she likes to hide Bubba's toys."

"The buff-and-orange one is Bubba, I take it?" Elise squatted beside the chowing cats and scratched Bubba on the neck. "Wow, his fur is really soft." Before rising again, she gave Diva equal time, then dusted cat hair from her hands and glanced at him. "So…any passwords I need to get logged on?"

"Naw. It should be up and running." He pried the lid off the can of coffee and watched over his shoulder as she headed out of the kitchen. Seeing another woman in Kelly's kitchen, petting her cats, hadn't been as strange or out of place as he'd thought it might. What did that mean? Was he finally moving past his wife's death? How could he be when he still felt such a powerfully hollow ache in his soul when he thought of her?

And just how many scoops of coffee had he put in the filter while his mind wandered?

Jared groaned and eyed the grounds already in the basket, added one more scoop for good measure and started the pot brewing. When he reached the guest room, Elise had a message board open on his computer, and he pulled a chair over to the desk to join her. "Whatcha got?"

She tapped a few keys, and the screen changed. "This is the website that Kim told us about. There are lots of subgroups depending on what you are interested in learning about or getting help with. Depression, grief, single parenting, missing children, divorce, various support groups for medical conditions... It's a real hodgepodge."

"Looks like it," he said reading over her shoulder, trying to ignore the tantalizing fruity scent of her hair.

"I browsed the site, getting a feel for it for several nights, then the other day I posted about Grace's death in the hospital to both the grief group and the Parents Without Children discussion. Turns out the Parents Without Children board is mostly used by people who don't see their kids anymore because of divorce, but a few have had kids that died or were kidnapped or ran away."

Elise clicked a link to open that discussion page. "See, here it is. I had a few replies, most of them just commiserating and offering condolences, but one lady said that her sister had lost a baby right after birth a couple years ago." She opened that reply, and pointing to the screen, she faced him. "And get this...she was at the same hospital as me. Pine Mill Community Hospital."

Jared sat back in his chair, stunned. "Wow. This is eerie."

"And when I did a search for infant death rates, I found an article about another couple in Pine Mill whose baby had died just after birth. It's like an epidemic in that town! Three babies in just a couple years. And there could be more for all we know." Her eyes blazed with fervor, and her voice echoed her passion.

"Just being a devil's advocate here. Three babies in two years is tragic but...well, maybe it's not an unusual number. Did you find any stats on infant mortality rates?"

She sighed and faced the screen again. "Yeah, and Louisiana's rate is higher than the national average. But...

my gut is telling me something is off. Something is wrong at that hospital, whether it's negligence or foul play or…I don't know what."

Jared steepled his fingers and tapped them against his chin as he mulled over the information. "Yeah, but you'd think if something bad was happening—whatever it was—that the health department or the state licensing board or law enforcement or *someone* would have stepped in by now."

"You'd think." She frowned and stared at the floor, clearly lost in her own turbulent thoughts.

He studied the screen, rereading the reply she'd opened. "Hey, you have four new replies. Want to check them out?"

She raised her head. "I do?" Grabbing the mouse, she clicked the first of the new messages. More condolences. The second reply was a link to an article from the same lady whose sister had lost her baby with the comment:

Here's more information from the Pine Mill newspaper about my sister's baby.

Elise followed the link to the article, and her shoulders drooped. "Oh, looks like the sister's baby is the same one I read about. This is the same article I found in my search."

"So…just two babies in two years?"

"Plus Kim's."

"But she was at a different hospital." His comment earned him a scowl.

"Yeah, but… Are you having second thoughts? Even two at one hospital is too many. I bet if I keep looking, I'll find more cases like mine and Kim's."

The desperation in her tone bothered him, and he studied her fiery expression. "To what end?"

She blinked. "Excuse me?"

"Why are you looking for more cases like yours?" he asked carefully, his tone low and gentle. "Is it a need to feel you aren't alone? A mission to discredit the hospital? Are you thinking of building a class-action lawsuit?"

She furrowed her brow, looking a bit poleaxed. "I…I don't know. I guess that depends on what I find out." Her expression turned angry, and she folded her arms over her chest. "Besides, you're the one who said I should arm myself with information. So I am. Why have you changed your tune?"

"I'm not saying I've changed my mind." He wrapped his fingers around her elbow and met her glare. "I just want to be sure you know what you're getting into. Are you prepared for what you might learn? Are you willing to take action if you find misfeasance or malpractice?"

Her anger faded, her expression softening to despondency. She opened her mouth and closed it again without answering. With a sigh, she turned back to the computer and stared at the screen.

Jared watched her, his heart aching for her. He regretted having encouraged her to undertake what could end up being a painful and fruitless search for answers. Maybe there was no good answer to why her baby died. At least he could blame the drunk driver for taking Kelly from him.

After a minute, she moved her hand listlessly to the mouse. Her expression downcast and discouraged, she clicked open the next message to her. More condolences— along with a phone number to call if she wanted to buy insurance. *Sheesh.* Some people.

The subject line of the last reply read, "Your baby." Elise opened the message, and Jared read over her shoulder again.

Check your email. I may have information about your baby.

The message was signed MysteryMom.

"Huh." She shifted on her chair and cast a glance to him. "What do you suppose…?"

He shrugged. "Check your email." While she navigated to a new web page and accessed her email account, he pulled his chair closer to the desk so that he was beside her.

Elise scrolled through advertisements for refinancing her mortgage, fliers from stores and jokes from friends until she found the email from MysteryMom.

She opened the email and leaned closer to the screen to read.

Dear Elise, I read your post on the Parents Without Children message board with a heavy heart. Losing a child is every mother's worst nightmare, and the last thing I'd ever want is to add to your pain. But the circumstances of your story rang familiar to me, and I took the liberty of doing some digging. I have powerful contacts with access to reliable information about birth records and have made it my mission to help mothers like you—and I do think I can help you. Not wanting to raise false hope for you, I triple-checked my information before contacting you.

Elise, my sources tell me that your baby might be alive.

Chapter 4

Elise froze. She stared at the message while a numbing disbelief swept through her. With an odd buzzing in her ears, she read the email again. And again. It really said what she thought. Was Gracie *alive?*

A strangled noise between a gasp and a whimper rasped from her throat.

"Oh, my God," Jared groaned. "Ignore it, Elise. Just delete it. Some people are just cruel beyond belief."

His voice roused her from her stupor, and a jolt of adrenaline rushed to her head, clearing the fog of shock. In its wake, her entire body revived with turbulent chaos. Her limbs shook, her stomach roiled, her head spun. She cast a confused glance at Jared. "What?"

He waved a hand at the screen in disgust. "Some crackpot is just yanking your chain, playing on your emotions. You watch. The next thing he'll send you is a request for money to help him locate your baby. If it's not a scam, then it's some jerk who gets off on giving desperate people false hope."

She fought for the breath to speak. "You…don't think it's real?"

"No way." He met her gaze and frowned. "Wait, you're not taking this seriously, are you? The guy didn't even sign his name."

"Not a guy. A woman. MysteryMom," she rasped. A chill settled in her bones, and she shuddered.

Jared grasped her upper arms, pulled her to her feet and into his arms. "Dear God, look at you. You're shaking." He wrapped her in a warm hug and rubbed her back. "It's okay. I know this is upsetting. Don't let this guy get to you."

She curled her fingers into his shirt and fought to steady her breathing. "B-but…what if it's real? M-maybe Grace *is* alive."

"Ah, Elise, don't…" Disappointment and concern weighted his tone.

Her mind raced, hyped up on the adrenaline and the possibilities MysteryMom's email created. Common sense told her Jared was likely right. The chances that Grace was still alive were remote. The odds that this "MysteryMom" was a con artist were high.

But a voice in her brain wouldn't let her discount the email out of hand. A maternal instinct deep inside screamed through the doubts that if there was even a hint that Gracie was alive somewhere, she had to do everything in her power to find her daughter and bring her home.

Dragging in a fortifying breath, she pushed back from Jared's embrace. Still clutching his shirtfront, she held him at arm's length and raised her eyes to his. "What would you do if it were Isabel?"

He tensed and scowled. "That's not—"

"No, think about it. If Isabel were kidnapped and the police told you they were certain she was dead and to give up ever finding her—"

A look of horror darkened his face, and he recoiled. "Elise, don't be—"

"Then you got an anonymous email saying she *was* alive—"

Jared sighed heavily and took a step back from her, rubbing his face with his hands. "It's not the same."

"You'd do everything you could to find her, wouldn't you?"

He gave her a disgruntled scowl. "Of course, but we're not talking about—"

"And I have to believe this MysteryMom is right, even if all practical sense says it's impossible. If Grace is out there, I have to find her!" Her heart thumped a wild cadence as hope grabbed the coattails of her determination and swelled in her chest.

Grace. Alive.

The idea was staggering. Exhilarating. Terrifying.

Overwhelmed by the implications, Elise swayed and collapsed in the desk chair. "If it's true...I—I don't even know where to begin. I—"

A maelstrom of conflicting emotions ravaged her, clogging her throat and pricking her eyes with tears.

Jared blew out a breath and sat in the chair beside her. "I'd say the first step is to reply to MysteryMom and get more details. Ask her who her sources are, what information led her to her conclusion. Ask her for credentials you can check out."

She turned to him, blinking to clear her vision. "Does this mean...you believe it could be true? You've changed your mind?"

He reached for her hands and folded them between

his. "It means you're right. If I thought there was even a remote chance Isabel were alive, I'd move mountains to find her." His eyes darkened, and he furrowed his brow. "I can't say I'm happy about this, but if you pursue this, I'm behind you one hundred percent. I'll do whatever I can to help."

Elise flipped her hands and laced her fingers with his, clinging to him as if he were her lifeline, her only connection to Grace. "Thank you."

Elise left shortly after that, assuring Jared that though she was still shocked by MysteryMom's email, she would be fine tonight. If only she was as certain of the same as she convinced him she was.

When she got home, she pulled the email up on her laptop and hit the reply button.

Who are you? What information do you have? How do I know I can believe you or trust your sources? If this is a joke, you are one sick puppy.

She sent the message and was logging in to the Parents Without Children message board when a bell sound told her she had a new email. Returning to her email program, she found a notice from her internet server claiming her reply to MysteryMom was undeliverable. "The addressee's mailbox is full," she read aloud.

Sighing her frustration, she returned to the message board and posted, "To MysteryMom—You have my attention, but my reply to you bounced. What's your game?"

She read a couple more commiserating replies to her original post and pushed away from her laptop to start getting ready for bed. Not that she thought she'd get any sleep, but she had to be at work early the next morning for a staff meeting. She would give sleep her best shot.

Brooke was already curled in a ball at the foot of her bed, sleeping soundly, and she stroked the tabby's fur as she made her way to the bathroom. While she brushed her teeth, her mind turning over the tantalizing possibility that Grace was alive, she heard a chime from her computer. Curious what had popped up, she wiped her mouth and crossed the room to her laptop. An instant message window from the discussion board website had appeared in the bottom corner of her screen.

She sat down and read.

No game. I'm your friend. I think I can help you, but you'll have to trust me. —MysteryMom

Elise's pulse tripped, and she dropped heavily onto her desk chair. This was her chance to grill MysteryMom for information. Quickly, she tapped out a reply and hit the send button.

Trust you? I don't even know who you are.

A few seconds later, MysteryMom answered.

I'm afraid I can't tell you who I am. It would jeopardize my ability to continue my work on behalf of single mothers. Please believe that I am your friend, not a prankster. —MysteryMom

Elise scowled and typed, What work? You mentioned reliable sources gave you the information about my daughter. Who are your sources? How do I know your information is credible?

MysteryMom replied, I have contacts in all levels of local and federal law enforcement. In recent years, I've made it my mission, my purpose, to reunite children with their parents. It is my passion to do this work on behalf of single mothers. I have kids of my own, and I know the love a mother has for her child.

Elise's fingers hovered over her keyboard as she considered her reply. She wanted desperately to believe MysteryMom could help her, could prove to her that there had been a horrific mistake at the hospital after Grace was born. Had Grace been accidentally switched with another baby? It seemed unlikely with all the safety protocols in place at hospitals these days. And yet…

Elise typed, So what do you suspect happened to my daughter? What makes you think she is alive? What evidence do you have?

MysteryMom answered, Your case is a bit different from the others I've worked on. Usually I find a missing parent, but your post to the message board reminded me of a case I'd read about here in Texas. I asked my sources to do a little leg work, and we think we may be on to something big involving the hospital where your daughter was born.

Big… like what?

We're investigating the staff there and in some other hospitals in Louisiana.

For malpractice? A class action lawsuit? What?

It's best I don't say anything more until I have confirmation of the facts. I need more information from you.

Warning bells sounded in Elise's head, and she scowled. If MysteryMom asked for financial information, her social security number or other key facts that could lead to identity theft, Elise would know the woman—if, in fact, MysteryMom was even a woman—was a fraud, preying on her vulnerability as a grieving mother.

Elise responded, What kind of information?

MysteryMom asked, Were you given any drugs to put you to sleep following the birth of your baby?

Elise gasped, remembering the injection the nurse had put in her IV despite her protests. It was while she'd been in her drug-induced sleep that Grace had died. The back of Elise's neck prickled.

She answered quickly, Yes, I was.

Did you ever see your baby again after you were told she'd died?

Nausea swamped Elise's gut. MysteryMom's questions cut right to the heart of the issues that had bothered Elise the most about Grace's death.

Elise typed her response. No. They told me her body had already been sent to the morgue. I was devastated...hysterical over her death, and they kept me sedated until right before I was released from the hospital. I had a closed-casket funeral.

What reason were you given for her death?

Elise explained what she'd been told about Grace's unexplained heart failure and the hospital's lack of sufficient critical-care facilities for newborns.

MysteryMom didn't reply for several tense moments. Finally Elise typed, Does all this tell you anything? What does it mean?

It follows the pattern we've uncovered.

Elise's breath backed up in her lungs as she reread the reply. Pattern? The term implied numerous cases similar to hers. Could it be that something more than tragic coincidence tied her loss to cases like the Harrisons' baby and the other couple in Pine Mill she'd read about?

Elise asked, How many other women have you heard from?

I haven't personally worked any other cases like yours. But with your permission, I'll give your information to my contact who is working a similar case.

Elise chewed her lip. Did she dare venture down this path? Was she asking for trouble trusting MysteryMom or could MysteryMom help her work a miracle? She glanced at the copy of the ultrasound picture that she kept on her bedside table. Really, there was no question. As she'd told Jared, if even a slight chance of finding Grace alive and getting her daughter back existed, it was worth the risk. You have my permission.

She spent the next twenty minutes answering Mystery-Mom's questions about the exact day and time of Grace's birth, her birth weight and length. When asked about identifying birthmarks or other details that might help in the search for Grace, Elise described the small pear-shaped red mark she'd seen on Grace's shoulder.

Then MysteryMom replied, I need to go. I'll catch you up on what I find out in a couple days. Let's meet back here, same time on Sunday night.

All right. In the meantime, what can I do to help?

Sit tight. Be patient. Give my investigators the time and space they need to look into this. Okay?

Elise frowned. She didn't like the idea of sitting on the sidelines when there was so much at stake. She started typing, What if I just ask around about—

Before she could finish her reply, the star by Mystery-Mom's user ID disappeared, indicating she'd logged off. Sighing her frustration, Elise deleted her question and scrolled through their exchange. The same phrases jumped out at her again and buzzed through her brain. *Contacts in law enforcement. Follows the pattern. I've made it my mission.*

Elise sat back in her chair and realized she was shaking. The idea that Grace was alive, that she could actually get her daughter back, filled her with dizzying joy and a fiery determination and purpose. She would find out the truth about what happened to Grace, no matter what it took.

I've made it my mission, too.

Chapter 5

Elise couldn't wait a week for the next grief-support meeting to talk to Jared about her exchange with MysteryMom. The next morning after her staff meeting at the newspaper, she phoned Jared's house and left a message with his mother, who was filling in as babysitter while Michelle was sick. Her next call was to her brother, Michael.

"Are you sitting down?" she asked him.

"Why? What's up?"

"Grace might not be dead."

A brief silence followed in which she pictured Michael's stunned expression.

"What are you talking about? How is that possible?"

She filled him in on everything that had transpired in the past few weeks, including meeting the Harrisons, posting on the Parents Without Children message board and MysteryMom's shocking announcement. When she was finished, she waited for him to comment.

"Well?" she nudged.

"You can't be taking this whack job seriously, can you? You had a funeral. You buried Grace, Elise. All the wishing in the world is not going to bring her back."

His blunt disbelief gouged at her heart. "But what if she never really died? MysteryMom asked if I'd ever actually seen her body, and it sank in that I hadn't. I'd been mourning the fact I hadn't had a chance to say goodbye, but I'd never let myself believe that it could mean she wasn't really dead."

"Elise, she's dead. Hospitals don't make mistakes about that. They might make mistakes in diagnoses or amputate the wrong leg sometimes, but dead is pretty cut-and-dried."

"But MysteryMom implied there could be—"

"Elise, stop. I love you, and I know how much losing your baby hurt you, but this is crazy!"

"Do you?"

"Do I what?"

"Do you have any idea how much losing Grace hurt me? You never call to check on me, and heaven forbid you visit. Michael, you're all the family I have, and—"

"Oh, here we go again," he interrupted. "Look, I don't have a lot of time right now. I'm sorry this person has fed you this pipe dream, but that's all it is. Don't buy into it. Don't torture yourself with false hopes."

"But—"

"Bye, Elise." The line clicked dead in her ear.

She gritted her teeth and shoved down the disappointment that her only family could be so unsupportive. Maybe he meant well, but his lack of faith still hurt.

But Michael had had his feelings betrayed by their parents, too. He'd been shifted around from one foster home to the next and learned to guard his heart and hoard his trust like she had.

Her thoughts drifted to Jared, how he'd warned her MysteryMom could be a crank, as well. But even if he hadn't completely changed his mind about MysteryMom, he'd come around enough to support Elise in pursuing the possibility Grace was alive. She appreciated his backing more than he might ever know.

Jared's support meant even more to her the next Thursday night when she explained the turn of events to the grief-support group. After laying out the gist of what MysteryMom had claimed, she glanced from one face to the next around the circle. Expressions ranged from dubious concern to scoffing dismissal.

"Elise…" Joleen began, and by her tone, Elise knew she was about to be cautioned again about the unlikelihood that MysteryMom's assertions had any merit.

She held up a hand. "I know what you're going to say. I know how it sounds, but if there's a chance it is true, I have to follow up on it."

"Sometimes our grief is so great that we create alternate realities," Joleen said, clearly picking her words carefully, "or build our hope around fantasies that have no basis."

Elise sighed her frustration, and Jared, who had sat quietly beside her as she made her case, reached over and took her hand. He gave her fingers a squeeze of support, and her agitation calmed enough to hear Joleen out.

"Denial and bargaining are steps in the grieving process, but I'd be remiss if I didn't advise you to let go of this. You'll only prolong the healing process and hurt yourself more by indulging in this wild goose chase."

Tears of disappointment stung her eyes, and she blinked them back. Shifting her attention to the Harrisons, Elise asked, "What would you do?"

Greg shook his head and waved her off. "I don't want to speculate."

"Kim? If it turns out that Grace is really alive, it could mean your baby didn't really die, either."

Kim gasped and stared at her with an expression that was half horror and half hope.

"Elise, don't." Joleen's tone was firm and unyielding. "I may not be able to talk you out of following this destructive path, but do not sabotage Kim's or any other member's healing by poisoning her with false hope. If you do, I'll have to ask you to leave the group."

Stunned by Joleen's ultimatum, Elise opened her mouth, but words didn't come. She scanned the faces around the circle. Some seemed disappointed in her, others hostile. Jared gave her a penetrating look that begged her to drop the subject.

Clearly the bomb she'd dropped on the group had been emotional and controversial. She'd expected a strong reaction, but she'd hoped at least a few of the group's members would be supportive of her decision to trust MysteryMom and search for Grace.

Sharp-edged rejection and betrayal sliced through her, every bit as dispiriting as when her father had dumped her and Michael in a foster home and walked away. Pulling her hand from Jared's, she rose from her chair, her legs shaking.

"Elise?" Jared sat straighter, worry etched in his brow.

"I...h-have to go," she croaked.

"Elise, don't leave. Please." Joleen's expression had softened, and she motioned toward Elise's empty chair. "I'm sorry if I sounded harsh, but my job is to facilitate a healthy and productive conversation in managing our grief. I just can't, in good conscience, condone what I honestly believe is a counterproductive, even dangerous, mind-set on your part."

Elise backed toward the door. "I understand. No hard feelings, but…this is…it's something I have to do."

With that, she turned and hurried through the corridor of the church and toward the exit. She heard the scrape of a chair in the meeting room and the pounding of running feet behind her.

"Elise, wait."

She paused, hand on the door handle, tears stinging her sinuses, and let Jared catch up to her. "Everyone thinks I'm nuts for buying into MysteryMom's theory and pursuing her contentions. My brother called it a pipe dream."

Jared put a hand on her shoulder and turned her to face him. Cupping her chin with his palm, he stroked her cheek with his thumb. "I don't think you're nuts."

"Really? The other day, when I read that first email from MysteryMom, you said—"

"I know what I said. And I still have a few doubts about this whole crazy scenario. But…" He pulled her into a firm embrace, pressing a kiss to the top of her head. "I've thought a lot about what you asked me the other night. In your position, I'd absolutely do the same thing."

Elise's heart swelled. His admission was just the confirmation she needed to quiet her doubt demons. "Thank you."

"For what? I haven't done anything."

"Yes, you have. You've done more for me than you could imagine by supporting me in this." She tipped her head back and met his gaze. "I was beginning to question my own sanity."

He finger-combed her hair away from her face, then skimmed his knuckles along her jaw. His touch sent a heady sensation spinning through her. Her fingers tightened their hold on his shirt, and her breath stuttered from her lungs. She hadn't been held like this by a man in so long. After discovering her last boyfriend was married and had no intention of leaving his wife, the idea of investing her emotions in any kind of intimacy scared her. Her father, her foster families, her lover. She'd been burned too many times to allow anyone else close.

Then she'd fallen in love with the child growing inside her. Losing Grace had felt like the greatest betrayal of all. Fate had taunted her with the precious bond of motherhood, only to snatch it away in a soul-shattering instant.

She knew growing attached to Jared when she was so vulnerable was risky. But at that moment, she needed to revel in the warmth of his friendship. She needed to feel she wasn't alone.

"Do you want to go get a bite to eat?" he said, his voice a lulling murmur. "You can catch me up on what you've heard from MysteryMom."

"That would be a short conversation. When we chatted by instant message on Sunday, she didn't have much to report yet."

He hummed an acknowledgment. "When are you supposed to be in touch with her again?"

"Perhaps tonight, if she can get free. She said not to panic if I didn't hear from her. She promised to be online Friday if she got tied up tonight."

"I'd like to be there when you IM with her next time."

"We're not IM-ing until ten. Isn't that kinda late for—Mmm…" She sighed blissfully as Jared massaged the back of her neck with his fingers. She could feel her tension seeping from her taut muscles and leaving her weak and pliant in his hands.

"Late for…?" he prompted.

She rolled her head to the side, relishing the deep rub as he worked his way to the base of her skull. She peered up at him from half-shuttered eyes. "I don't remember. Lord, that feels so good. Don't stop. Ever."

A low rich chuckle rumbled from his chest. "Like that, do you?"

Elise closed her eyes. "Mmm-hmm."

"Can you access the IM from my computer?"

"I think so. We use the message board IM on the website I showed you last week."

Jared's hand stilled on her neck, and she opened her eyes, curious why he'd stopped the relaxing massage. His focus was riveted on her mouth, and his expression reflected an inner battle. He wanted to kiss her. She saw that much in the desire that darkened his eyes. But something held him back.

"Jared..." She could only manage a rasp, as longing and doubt squeezed her lungs.

Tightening his hold around the back of her head, he drew her closer. She held her breath as he brushed his lips against hers. Softly, tentatively at first, as if seeking permission. Sweet sensations washed through her, and she couldn't help the half moan, half sigh that he took as an invitation to deepen the kiss. Angling his mouth, he drew on her lips with a gentle persuasion and exquisite finesse.

She canted forward, leaning into him, into the kiss. Her world narrowed to the two of them and that moment. Any reservations she'd had fled, and a pleasant lethargy filled her body.

When he broke the kiss, he didn't back away. Instead, he rested his forehead against hers, closed his eyes and grew very still. Elise was grateful for the moment to collect herself. But when he continued to hold her without speaking, she sensed what was wrong.

"So...I'm guessing I am the first woman you've kissed since Kelly died."

He drew a deep, slow breath and released it. "Yeah."

"And it was…weird for you?"

He opened his eyes and levered back just far enough to meet her gaze. His brow furrowed as if he were mulling over her question. "Actually…what's weird is…it wasn't weird."

"No?"

"In fact it was…pretty great." He hiked up a corner of his mouth, and a dimple pocked his cheek.

Elise's pulse fluttered. "Then you're okay? You were quiet for so long I thought maybe…"

"I was regretting it?"

Her stomach swooped. "I was going to say something else but…do you regret it?"

He caressed the side of her face, and his smile grew. "No. I was praying that I hadn't offended you or scared you off. I know you're vulnerable right now, and I don't want to pressure you or take advantage of you."

His consideration touched her but didn't surprise her. Jared had already shown her in many ways that he understood her needs and her confused emotions. His patience and thoughtfulness earned him a little more of her respect and gratitude.

But consideration was not what she wanted in the wake of his earthshaking kiss. The crackle of her nerve endings told her how long it had been since she'd burned for a man's kiss. She slid her arms around his neck and tipped a coy grin his direction. "Did I complain?"

He lifted one eyebrow. "Hmm. In that case…" He tugged her close again and covered her lips with another toe-curling kiss.

Elise let herself sink into the sweet oblivion. She didn't stop to analyze what was happening. Something so elemental required no explanation. The spark of attraction she'd sensed between them had needed only a little help to be fanned into a bright blaze.

Jared stroked a hand down her back, his fingertip strumming the ridge of her spine and heightening the tingle already shooting through her. When his caress reached her waist, he slipped his hand beneath the hem of her sweater. The heat of his fingers against her bare skin sent shock waves to her core. When she trembled, he tightened his hold on her and pulled her flush against his taut muscles. Heat radiated from him in waves, cocooning her, and for a few moments, she was able to shut out the icy cold of grief, the uncertainty of her future and the ache of loss.

A door closed somewhere down the church corridor, and the click of footsteps on the linoleum floor reminded her where she was and that their privacy was an illusion. She jerked back from him, and Jared reluctantly released her.

"Elise?"

She pressed a hand to her swollen lips and drew a slow breath for composure. "Do you have decaf coffee at your house?"

He blinked and scrubbed a hand down his cheek. "I think so."

"Then I'll follow you in my car, and I'll catch you up on my week while we wait for MysteryMom to get online."

At Jared's house, his mother filled them in on Isabel's dinner and nap status, and while Jared walked his mom to her car, Elise joined Isabel on the living-room floor. On impulse, Elise had brought her camera inside, and she snapped a couple pictures as Jared's daughter gnawed on a wooden block and blinked her wide blue eyes at her visitor.

"Hi, Isabel. Do you remember me?" She picked up the

stuffed elephant beside her and walked it across the floor to Isabel's foot. "Elephant's gonna kiss you!" She made a silly smacking noise as she pressed the soft toy to the baby's cheek.

Isabel chuckled, then crawled closer to Elise. Grabbing fistfuls of Elise's sweater, Jared's daughter pulled herself up to her knees and studied Elise with an earnest expression. "Kee?"

Elise laughed. "So you do remember me, huh?"

Isabel plopped down on her diapered bottom and clapped her hands. "Kee-kee."

"As a matter of fact…" She reached for her purse, which she'd deposited on the sofa and dug in the bag for the snack pack of cookie bites she'd saved from her lunch. "Do you like shortbread?"

Isabel saw the foil packet, and her eyes glowed. "Kee!"

When Jared returned from the driveway, Elise had Isabel on her lap, and they were sharing a snack of shortbread cookies.

"And they say the way to a man's heart is through his stomach," she said around a mouthful. "I hate to think how your daughter might have rejected me if not for my bakery offerings."

"Ah, yes. My girl's a little cookie monster." Jared joined them on the sofa and held his hands out to Isabel. She refused to go to him. "Well, well. Somebody has made a new friend. You have a great rapport with her."

Elise grinned and hugged Isabel. "As long as the cookie supply lasts anyway."

But even before the cookies ran out, Isabel began whining and rubbing her eyes with sticky fingers.

"Gee, princess, it's kinda early for bed." Jared scratched his chin and gave Isabel a thoughtful look. "If I put you down now, you'll be up before the birds. Which means I will be, too."

Isabel rubbed a cookie-covered hand on her ear and wrinkled her nose as she fussed.

"Could she be coming down with something?" Elise asked. "I know I like to go to bed early when I feel bad."

"Well, Mom did say she's been cranky today and has a stuffy nose."

Isabel's whine escalated to a cry, and Jared shoved off the couch. "Okay, sweetie, let's get a bath."

Elise's heart melted hearing Isabel's mewling cry. "Want help?"

"Thanks, I got it." He must have seen her disappointment, because he hesitated. "But...you can rock her to sleep in a few minutes if you want."

Elise smiled. "I'd love that."

The next afternoon, Elise sat at her computer at the newspaper office reviewing the pictures she'd taken at a political rally earlier that morning. The task was taking twice as long as usual because her mind kept straying to her plans for that evening. MysteryMom had been a no-show the night before, so she and Jared had made arrangements to have dinner out then head back to his house to wait for MysteryMom's update at his computer.

Elise's mind was on Jared's kiss at the church the night before, her body humming with the same energy she'd experienced as he held her, when the editor-in-chief stopped by her desk, a cup of coffee in his hand. "Norris, Russell tells me his feature on the new art exhibit for next Saturday's edition hit a snag and needs to be bumped another week. This means there's room for your photo essay and feature piece, if you're still interested."

She sat straighter in her chair. "Yes, absolutely."

"Did you come up with any more ideas that weren't as lame-brained as your others?"

Cringing mentally at his critical attitude, she pulled out the notepad she'd been keeping her ideas on. "Well, the new library branch will be opening—"

"Boring."

"Uh, local breast cancer survi—"

"Been done. Often."

She took a deep breath to tamp down her frustration. "I heard about a man in town who was at Normandy on D-day. He's in a nursing home, but he's still quite lucid and according to his family has lots of stories about the war."

He sipped his coffee, and she held her breath.

"I like that."

A flutter of excitement stirred in her gut.

"But…"

She deflated.

"Russell can do that story on Memorial Day. We'll get the geezer to tell us all about his friends that died."

She prickled at her boss's reference to a decorated war hero as a "geezer" but bit down on the cynical retort that formed on her tongue.

"What else ya got?"

She sighed. "That's about it for now, but I'll keep brain-storming, and—"

"You do that. I'll be in my office when you have your breakthrough." Mr. Grimes strolled away, slurping his coffee, and Elise gritted her teeth.

At least he'd given her the green light to do a photo essay and write a feature. That was progress. Unless he was just yanking her chain, telling her she could do the article then nixing all her ideas to shut her up.

Russell popped up in his cubicle like a groundhog and

peered over the partition. "Don't let him get to you. He gets off on being a jerk."

Raking her hair back with her fingers, she blew out a breath of irritation. "I know he does. But this chance is important to me. I don't want to blow it."

Russell glanced over his shoulder toward Grimes's office then back to Elise. "Listen, all of your ideas have been good ones. Really. Just wait. He'll be assigning me the library story in a couple weeks and make it look like it was his idea."

Elise grunted and rolled her eyes. "That doesn't help me now."

"You'll think of something. My advice? Make it something that matters to you. Your passion for the topic will come through in your writing and in how you present the topic to Grimes."

She nodded. "Thanks. I'll keep that in mind."

Russell gave her a wink and disappeared behind the cubicle wall.

Something that mattered to her... She bit the cap of her pen and tried to shove aside her annoyance with her boss so she could think. When her phone rang, she answered mechanically, her mind miles away.

"Hi, I hope it's okay that I called you at work." *Jared.*

The sound of his voice sent her heartbeat into overdrive. She dropped the pen she'd been gnawing and turned her back to the newsroom, as if it would afford her more privacy. "No...I mean, yes, it's okay. What's up?"

"Well, Isabel's temperature for one. I hate to leave her when she's sick, so...about tonight..."

Disappointment plucked at her along with concern for Isabel. "I understand. Have you taken her to a doctor? What's wrong with her?"

"Probably just an ear infection. We're on the way to see the pediatrician now."

"Another time then? For dinner, I mean."

"Actually, if you're still game, I have a lasagna in my freezer that my mom brought over a few days ago. We can eat here, watch a movie, and I can keep an eye on the princess."

The princess. She smiled at his pet name for his daughter. "Sounds lovely. What can I bring?"

Elise hung up a few minutes later, having settled the new plans, and as she spun back to her computer, a copy of her ultrasound picture of Grace caught her eye. Her breath hitched, and the usual pang of longing and sadness bit her. Was anyone taking Grace to the doctor when she had an earache? Oh, what she'd give to be the one sitting up with her daughter when she was ill! Assuming MysteryMom was right about her being alive...

She shifted restlessly in her desk chair. Waiting for answers from MysteryMom was one of the hardest things she'd ever done. Elise needed to *do,* not sit on the sidelines. Especially something as important as—

She gripped the armrests of her chair as a half-formed idea popped into her head. Could she write an exposé on the questionable infant deaths? Without having fully decided what angle she'd take, she shot out of her seat and hurried to Mr. Grimes's office.

"I have an idea—" she started before realizing he was on the phone.

He held up a finger to say "wait a minute" and finished his call.

She gripped the edge of his door, and as she waited, doubts assailed her. MysteryMom had asked her not to get involved, not to do anything to undermine her contact's investigation. If she went to the hospital half-cocked, asking questions, would she blow whatever work MysteryMom had done?

As Grimes hung up, he shot her an impatient look. "All right. Dazzle me."

"I—" Her mouth went dry. How could she frame her piece in a way that wouldn't raise red flags but would still allow her to go behind the scenes at Pine Mill Hospital and snoop around?

Grimes steepled his fingers and rocked back in his desk chair. "Well?"

"I want to do…s-something at Pine Mill Hospital."

He stared at her blankly. Blinked slowly.

Okay, Elise, get it together. If you're going to get the okay for this assignment you have to sell it.

She cleared her throat. "With all the debate about health care in the nation recently, I was thinking I'd do a piece about a day in the life at a small-town hospital. So many small hospitals are struggling financially and…" He lifted one eyebrow, which she took as encouragement. "Just one day at any hospital is kind of symbolic of life as a whole…" Her idea began to jell, and as she warmed to it, her voice strengthened and passion infused her proposal. "I mean… life begins at a hospital in the maternity department, and we pass through again when we meet obstacles or have celebrations along the way…illness, accidents, the birth of our children—" *And the loss of our children.* She struggled to keep her composure as she plowed on. "And eventually, many times, we go to a hospital to die. The circle of life, right?"

She was drawing a breath to continue, when he waved a dismissive hand.

"Okay. Do it. Bye."

Elise blinked. "Really? I can do that story?"

"Are you deaf? Did I stutter?"

Excitement and relief pumped through her, and she flashed him a broad grin, ignoring his sarcasm. "Thank you!"

"I need it on my desk in a week."

A week. Her stomach clenched. She had to pull together a plan and get to work *pronto*. Step one, call the hospital administration and arrange access behind the scenes for her photo shoot and interviews with key employees. Dr. Arrimand, for one.

She dropped into her desk chair and pressed a hand to her swirling gut.

For the first time in more than a year, she was going back to the scene where her nightmare had begun.

Chapter 6

"Are you sure this is a good idea? Should I come with you?" Jared asked later in the week, his voice coming from her cell phone, which she'd set to speaker. Even when he wasn't there in person, the deep richness of his voice resonated inside her, kindling a tingling heat at her core.

Elise smiled. His concern for her helped calm the butterflies that swooped in her gut as she pulled into a parking spot at Pine Mill Hospital. "I'll be fine. Besides, I'm already at the hospital. I'm meeting with the chief administrator in ten minutes. He thinks my photo essay will be a great PR plug for the hospital, and he was thrilled to give me open access to any department I want to see."

"Just…be careful. Call me when you're done."

She could hear Isabel babbling in the background, and she felt a little catch in her chest. She drew a deep breath for courage and gathered her purse and camera bag from the seat beside her. "I will."

After locking her car, Elise stowed her keys in her purse and strode toward the front door, buffeted by a cool autumn wind. The volunteer at the information desk directed her to the office of the hospital administrator, George Bircham. The silver-haired man, who wore a suit that looked like he'd owned it since the 1970s, greeted her warmly and conducted the first several minutes of the tour himself. They'd visited the pediatric hall and the radiology lab first, while Elise clicked pictures and scribbled notes. Next, Mr. Bircham led her to the E.R. A shiver chased down her spine as she remembered entering the emergency room months ago, doubled over in pain as her contractions peaked. From the E.R., she'd been rushed upstairs to Labor and Delivery just in time for Grace's arrival.

"And unlike big-city hospitals where you may wait hours to be seen, our emergency-care department boasts an average wait of only eleven minutes!" the administrator bragged as his pager sounded. "I'm sorry, Ms. Norris. I have to answer this call." He flagged down a nurse who was leaving the cafeteria. "You work in Labor and Delivery, don't you?"

When the nurse nodded, Bircham introduced Elise and asked the nurse to show her around, let her take pictures and answer her questions.

"Thank you for your time," Elise said, shaking his hand then falling in step behind the nurse whose name tag identified her as Cheryl Watts.

Elise wiped sweat from her palms on her slacks as they rode the elevator to the second floor. When they reached Labor and Delivery, Cheryl led her to the nurses' station and introduced her to the nurses there. Elise snapped a couple pictures and asked a few innocuous questions to make the nurses feel more comfortable.

"What's going on here?" a male voice asked from behind her.

Her pulse jumped, and she nearly knocked over the coffee of one of the nurses as she spun to face the man in scrubs. *Dr. Arrimand.*

Would he recognize her? Remember her name?

Shoving down the swirl of nerves that danced through her, she stuck her hand out and pasted on a bright smile. "Elise Norris from the *Lagniappe Herald.* Mr. Bircham has granted me permission to photograph the behind-the-scenes operation here at Pine Mill for a feature article and photo spread about small-town hospitals."

He shook her hand and eyed her camera. "Bircham approved this?"

"Yes. I think he saw it as good promotion for the hospital. I'm planning a day-in-the-life piece."

The doctor lifted an eyebrow as if intrigued.

"I'd love to interview you for the article," she said as inspiration struck. Could she get any valuable information from him without arousing suspicion? She'd have to be careful, cagey.

"Dr. Arrimand, we're ready for you in delivery two."

Elise recognized the nurse who'd arrived to summon the doctor and flashed back to the minutes after Grace was born. She was the woman who'd injected her with the drug that had put her to sleep after only a brief time with Grace. When the nurse glanced toward Elise, the woman did a double take and frowned.

"On my way," Dr. Arrimand said. "I have to go now, but I can give you about ten minutes in around an hour."

"That's terrific. Thank you."

He started to walk away then turned back and aimed a finger at her. "I expect you to respect the patients' privacy. No pictures without their permission. Understand?"

"Absolutely." She could barely contain her relief as she watched him march down the hall. An interview with Dr. Arrimand was the next best thing to…

Her breath caught, and she hurried down the hall after the doctor. "Dr. Arrimand, wait!"

He paused and sent her an irritated look as she caught up to him. "I'd like to go into the delivery with you." Seeing a refusal coming from the darkening of his expression, she rushed on to explain, "The birth of a baby is so symbolic. I want to show how the hospital is there for the community from the beginning of life until the end and at major milestones along the way. I'll get the mother's permission, of course, and use the utmost professionalism and discretion in the angles I shoot."

"Dr. Arrimand!" the delivery-room nurse called from down the hall. She held a surgical gown out ready for the doctor to slip into.

"All right," he said, trotting away.

Elise followed at a jog, but was stopped at the door by the nurse. "You'll need sterile garb if you're coming in. The kits are on that shelf."

Finding the sterile coverings, Elise hastily donned the gown, shoe and hair covers, and a pair of latex gloves. When she entered the delivery room, the bright lights and antiseptic smell hit her with a cascade of memories. A tremor rose from deep in her core, and she fought the urge to flee.

The husband of the woman giving birth gave her a curious look. "What's with the camera?"

Seizing on the distraction and recalled to her reason for being there, she introduced herself and gave a quick summary of what she wanted to photograph. The couple agreed, and Elise began snapping pictures from the head of the bed.

Elise caught the moment Dr. Arrimand held the baby boy up for the couple to see for the first time and the moment the delivery nurse placed the swaddled infant in the mother's arms. Her hand trembled so badly as she photographed the family bonding that she was sure the pictures would be too blurry to use. Tears puddled in her eyes when the father bent to press a kiss on his new son's head.

She swallowed hard to clear the knot of emotion clogging her throat.

Oh, Grace, what happened to you?

"Congratulations." Her voice sounded choked as she set the camera aside and took out her notebook. "Do you have a name picked out?"

"Dillon Charles," the woman said, beaming proudly at the boy.

As Elise scribbled the name in her notes, the delivery nurse nudged her out of the way.

"Mom needs to rest, and we need to finish cleaning him up and give him a thorough health screening."

Elise held her breath, waiting to see if the mother was injected with any drugs. She watched as baby Dillon was passed to another nurse who placed a hospital ID on his ankle and laid him carefully in a clear bassinet labeled Baby Boy Thompson. Still no injection had been given to the mother. Elise was torn whether to follow the baby as he was rolled out of delivery to the nursery or stay with the mother to see what happened to her.

"When will the pictures be in the paper?" Dillon's father asked. "We want to be sure to get a copy…or ten."

Deciding what happened to the baby was the key to learning anything that would help find Grace, Elise backed toward the door, trying to keep the nurse with the baby in sight. "Uh…next weekend, I think. I—" She stepped into the hall in time to see the baby wheeled into the last room at the end of the corridor. "Thank you," she said in a rush, "for sharing your special moment with me…and our readers. I… Good luck."

She gave a little wave to the couple and hustled down the hall to the nursery. Through the plate glass window, she spotted the nurse unwrapping Dillon, carefully wiping him clean, and fitting him with a tiny diaper and blue cap. Next, she listened to his heart and lungs, and Elise clicked a few pictures through the glass. Lowering the camera, she watched the rest of the procedure until Dillon was returned to his bassinet and rolled into place next to the other babies. She chewed her lower lip with a strange sense of disappointment gnawing at her. Had she really been hoping to witness and document some egregious flaw in the delivery process? She would never want another baby placed in jeopardy the way Grace might have been, but how was she supposed to prove something was amiss at this hospital when everything she'd seen today seemed on the up-and-up?

She checked her watch and saw she had several minutes before her meeting with Dr. Arrimand, enough time to visit the morgue and ask a few questions. A chill shimmied through her. She dreaded the idea of seeing the morgue, but if her article was truly to cover the hospital's role in both the start and end of a person's life, a few pictures in the morgue were needed.

The coroner on duty, who introduced himself as Dr. Galloway, explained to her how he processed a body and which ones required an autopsy.

Clutching her pen so hard she thought it might break, Elise took notes on what he said. "Wh—what about babies? Are they handled any differently?"

The coroner gave her a sad smile. "Babies are always

sad cases, but no, they are treated the same as any other body we receive. Fortunately, the babies are few and far between. When we do get a child of any age, they stand out. That's a hard day at work."

"Can you tell me how many babies, newborns, you've had in the last two years?"

Dr. Galloway gave her an odd look, and she had to admit her question must have sounded morbid. "Only one or two off the top of my head. But Dr. Hambrick, the other coroner who works here, might have worked a case like that. Is it relevant to your article? I can look it up in our records if it's important."

Elise's nerves jangled, and she clutched her notepad against her chest like a shield. "Yes, please. I would like know."

He stepped over to a computer and logged in. "All babies or just newborns?"

"Just newborns." She bit her bottom lip as he scrolled through his records and sorted and filtered the information.

"Let's see…" He bent over the keyboard to study the results on his monitor. "In the last two years, we handled five babies that were less than a week old."

"Five?" Elise moved behind him to look over his shoulder at the screen. "Isn't that a lot?"

Dr. Galloway shrugged. "One seems like a lot to me."

"True."

He pointed to the monitor. "First one was stillborn, no autopsy run. The next three were significantly premature. No autopsies. And the last one…jeez, a one-week-old baby. Autopsy showed he died of shaken-baby syndrome."

Elise gasped. "How horrible!"

The coroner nodded. "I remember the case. The new mother was drunk at the time and couldn't get the baby to stop crying. Shook him so hard it caused brain damage and death. Dr. Hambrick had to testify at her trial. So sad."

Elise frowned. Where was Grace's record? "Are you sure that's all? Just those five?"

"Just those five?" He gave her a speculative glance. "A minute ago you said five was a lot."

"Well, it is…but…I just thought maybe…well, could that record be incomplete?"

"It's updated in real time. That's all the newborns under a week old that we handled."

Elise's head spun, and her knees shook so hard she had to sit down. The morgue had no record of Grace, with or without an autopsy. Was that more evidence the hospital had lied to her? Had given her false information about an autopsy being performed on Grace?

"Are you all right, ma'am?" Dr. Galloway narrowed a concerned look on her. "You look like you've seen a ghost."

"Oh, I…I just felt dizzy for a minute. I skipped lunch and…" Her voice trailed off as a new thought occurred to her.

Did the lack of a record on Grace support Mystery-Mom's theory that Grace was alive somewhere? Her pulse sped up, and a bubble of hope swelled in her chest.

"Can you print that page for me?"

He hesitated. "I'm not sure I—"

"Are you familiar with the Freedom of Information Act? By law, the public has a right to public records, including—"

He held up a hand to stop her. "But personal medical records are, by law, private. Since these records show only statistics, however, I guess it's okay. If you have a few minutes, I'll get it for you, but our printer is out of paper."

She checked her watch. She was due in Dr. Arrimand's office. "Can I stop back by and get it later? I'm interviewing Dr. Arrimand in just a few minutes."

Galloway's eyebrows shot up. "You managed to get an interview with Joe Arrimand?"

"Yes. Why?"

"He's not usually the talkative sort. Keeps to himself, doesn't socialize with the rest of the hospital staff much. And he's as busy as a one-legged man at a butt-kicking contest."

Elise had to chuckle at his simile. "I wouldn't have thought there were that many babies born here."

"Not just here. He also works at Crestview General and Clairmont Hospital."

Crestview. Where Kim had delivered her baby. A chill slithered through Elise as she processed the ramifications.

"Tell you what," he said. "I'll bring the copies to you. I'm headed out to dinner soon, so I'll stop by Dr. Arrimand's office with it."

With a grateful smile, she thanked Dr. Galloway for his assistance and hurried back upstairs to her meeting with Dr. Arrimand. She forced the new questions that buzzed through her brain to a back burner. She didn't need to be distracted or agitated as she interviewed Dr. Arrimand.

As she rode the elevator from the basement to the second floor, she checked her camera and discovered her memory card was full. Popping the card from its slot, she tucked it in her pocket and found a new one in her camera bag. She'd just clicked the new memory card in place when the elevator slid open.

Down the hall by the nursery's viewing window, a small crowd had gathered, laughing and cooing. Dillion's mother sat in a wheelchair in the middle of an adoring family, and his father received handshakes and slaps on the back.

Elise shoved aside her envy of the joyous occasion and

asked at the nurses' station for directions to Dr. Arrimand's office. The delivery nurse gave her a suspicious scowl, but Cheryl Watts escorted her down a back hall.

The doctor, still in his scrubs, greeted her more cordially than he had earlier and waved her toward a chair across from him. "I trust you're getting the information you need for your article, Ms. Norris. My staff tells me you've been taking lots of pictures."

"Well, photography is my first love and my regular assignment with the newspaper. But I was given special permission by my boss to write the accompanying article for this feature, as well, so that's the reason behind all the questions. I want to knock my boss's socks off, so that he'll trust me to do more features like this in the future."

Dr. Arrimand chuckled. "That's the spirit. How can I help you knock his socks off?"

She flipped open her pad to a fresh page and tapped her pen on it, thinking. As she had with the hospital administrator, Elise decided to start with few simple questions to put him at ease. "Tell me your favorite thing about your job. I mean…it must be so inspiring to be able to witness the miracle of new life every day, to see the joy of the parents and family…"

"Absolutely. That is the best part of the job." He went on to talk about a few of his favorite patients, the birth of his own children and the reason he chose obstetrics as a career. She asked him about his choice to work in the small-town hospital versus a larger hospital like the ones in Shreveport, New Orleans or Lagniappe.

"Well, I'm small-town born and raised. My father died when I was young, and my mother struggled to take care of us. We were as poor as dirt, but the town took care of us any way they could. I owe a lot to this town, and so in my own way, I'm paying back the folks who helped my family. Besides, I like living in Pine Mill, away from the crime and hustle and bustle."

Elise nodded, scribbling notes furiously. She furrowed her brow, debating the best way to phrase her next question. "Being a smaller hospital with less money, Pine Mill isn't able to afford some of the emerging technology and equipment. Do you find it frustrating having limited resources?"

He scoffed. "You make it sound like we're backward and out of date."

"Let me clarify. In the labor-and-delivery department, you don't have the critical-care facilities like St. Mary's in Lagniappe."

He turned up a palm. "And St. Mary's doesn't have the cutting-edge facilities to treat childhood cancer the way St. Jude does, and the Mayo Clinic has better facilities than a lot of places." He smiled. "There's always going to be a dog on the block with a bigger bone or a better doghouse. We do the best we can with what we have. Our patients get top-notch care for a hospital our size."

Elise opted not to press the issue, despite his politician-like deflection. She didn't want to raise undue suspicion about her hidden agenda. "Okay, we've talked about your favorite part of the job, helping bring babies into the world, but what about your least favorite?"

He laughed heartily. "Oh, that's easy. Paperwork." He motioned to his messy desk. "As you see I'm a bit behind in that department."

A knock on the door saved her from an awkward reply.

"Yes?" Dr. Arrimand called.

The door opened, and the nurse from the delivery room entered. "I'm sorry to interrupt." She cast a wary look toward Elise then hurried over to the doctor and bent at the waist to whisper in his ear.

The doctor's expression darkened, and he cut a quick, accusing look toward Elise. Had she not been watching the exchange with the nurse closely, she might have missed the telltale glance, but that brief sidelong glare told her she was the topic of the nurse's secret.

She sat forward in her chair, the nape of her neck tingling.

"You're sure?" Dr. Arrimand murmured in a low voice.

His nurse gave a quick, almost imperceptible nod.

"Okay, thank you, Helen." He leaned back in his chair, silently dismissing the nurse, and he turned back to Elise. The doctor was no longer smiling.

"Is everything all right?" she asked after several uncomfortable seconds of silence.

"Just fine." He leaned forward, bracing his weight on his folded arms, which he propped on his desk. His sudden shift felt aggressive, and Elise fought the urge to shrink back from his penetrating glare.

"Tell me something, Ms. Norris. What made you pick Pine Mill Hospital for the subject of your article? There are plenty of small hospitals in this corner of the state."

Adrenaline spiked in her, and her gut clenched. "Pine Mill Hospital seemed to be a fair representation of the kind of health care available in—"

"A fair representation based on what? Whose assessment?"

"Well, mine. I—"

"And what past experience do you have with our hospital?" He arched an eyebrow in query, his expression still stern.

Elise scrambled for an answer that wouldn't sound any alarms. What had the nurse told him that led him to grill her like this?

Her neck felt flushed. Her tongue dried, and when she

opened her mouth to speak, the words stuck in her throat. She paused long enough to swallow hard, aware the gesture gave away her nerves. She hated being the one on the hot seat.

She opted for honesty. He'd look her name up when she left anyway, if that wasn't what his nurse had already done. If she were to get caught in a lie, she'd cause more suspicion than being forthright…to an extent. "I was a patient here about a year ago."

"Is that so? Under what circumstances?"

She took a deep breath, gathering her composure. She needed to regain control of the interview. She was supposed to be the one asking the questions.

"How long have you worked at this hospital, Dr. Arrimand?"

"Twenty-one years. Why were you a patient here?" he volleyed back.

"I had a baby. Where did you work before coming to Pine Mill?"

His jaw tightened. "Boy or girl?"

"You didn't answer my question." Elise's heart was drumming so loud, she wondered if the doctor could hear it. He could probably see the frantic cadence as it hammered against her chest. "You also work at other small hospitals in the area. Is that right?"

Another knock sounded on the office door.

"What!" he barked to the visitor.

Dr. Galloway pushed open the door and stepped in. "Sorry to interrupt, Joe, but I promised these records to Ms. Norris."

"No problem." Dr. Arrimand's dark eyes stayed fixed on Elise. "We were finished here anyway."

Dr. Galloway held out the copies he'd made, and she

quickly stuffed them in the pocket of her camera bag, out of sight.

"Good luck with your article," the coroner said as he backed out of the office.

"Thank you." She forced a strained smile to her lips.

By the time she turned back to Dr. Arrimand, he'd risen behind his desk and folded his arms over his chest. "I'm afraid that's all the time I have, Ms. Norris."

Okay, she was getting the brush-off.

"Could we reschedule and finish the interview later?"

"That won't be necessary. I have nothing else to say." He stalked to his door and opened it. "You know the way out, don't you?"

And he was in a hurry to get rid of her. Interesting.

"I…yeah." She gathered her purse and camera bag, hiking both straps onto her shoulder as she made her way to the door. Maintaining her professionalism, she offered the doctor her hand to shake. "Thank you for your time."

He gave her fingers a perfunctory squeeze, flashed a false smile and opened the door wider.

Elise walked out, receiving a cool look from his delivery nurse, then headed for the elevator. Once the doors slid shut, she slumped against the back wall and released a deep breath. What had that been about? He'd morphed from amiable, if grudging, host to combatant in seconds. Because of whatever the nurse had told him.

Obviously they knew she'd had Grace there, and, quite possibly, they were concerned about a malpractice lawsuit. Or was there more to it than that? Did they realize Grace had died? Or rather that they'd *told* her Grace had died. She was more certain than ever that something nefarious, something *illegal* was going on at Pine Mill Hospital.

And Dr. Arrimand had a hand in it.

* * *

Elise hustled out to her car and put her camera bag and purse on the passenger seat next to her. As soon as she got home, she would post a notice on the Parents Without Children message board asking MysteryMom to contact her. MysteryMom's investigators needed to see the new information she had from the coroner, and Elise wanted MysteryMom to know about Dr. Arrimand's odd behavior. While the doctor's inhospitality didn't prove anything, every piece in this puzzle helped create a fuller picture.

She pulled out onto the rural highway and headed back to Lagniappe. The dashboard clock said it was still early enough for her to make it home by dinnertime. She could stop by Jared's, show him her pictures and get his opinion concerning the doctor's behavior.

And she could see Isabel before she went to bed. Her heart gave a joyful flutter. Jared's daughter had toddled her way into Elise's heart, and no one was more surprised than Elise. Not that Isabel wasn't precious and easy to love, but Elise had fallen head over heels for the pixie's slobbery grin and wide blue eyes. Somehow, instead of a painful reminder of her loss, Isabel was healing Elise's broken heart. And firing her resolve to find Grace. To find the truth that MysteryMom alluded to in her last email.

A loud *vroom* pulled her out of her deliberations, and she glanced in her rearview mirror to locate the source. A large silver pickup truck barreled down the road toward her. Judging from how rapidly the truck was catching up to her, she estimated the driver had to be pushing eighty miles per hour—a dangerous speed in most circumstances, but on this twisty two-lane road, such speed was deadly.

Gritting her teeth in disgust, she squeezed the steering wheel and prepared to take defensive maneuvers, if needed.

The idiot behind her might like to taunt death, but she had no desire to die today because of his foolishness.

Especially not now that she'd met Jared and Isabel.

The unbidden thought startled her, along with the gooey warmth that puddled in her gut when she thought of the father and daughter. Spending time with Jared and his daughter made her happy. For the first time since losing Grace, she had found the kind of joy that made her want to see what the new day would bring. She looked forward to the next time she could play with Isabel and share a bowl of popcorn and warm snuggles on the couch with Jared.

Elise chewed her bottom lip. Being happy was good, right? Then why did the idea of growing closer to the father and daughter fill her with such trepidation?

Her heart stutter-stepped. *The more you care, the more you have to lose.*

Behind her, the silver truck gunned its engine again and pulled alongside her. She sent a glare to the driver for his recklessness. Through the tint of his windows, all she could tell was that he was a heavyset man who wore a ball cap and dark sunglasses. He turned his head and met her stare.

Then veered his truck into the side of her car. Metal crunched and groaned. Her car lurched toward the shoulder.

Elise gasped and battled the steering wheel, keeping her car on the road. Barely.

The truck swerved again, crashing into her, shoving her until her right tires left the highway.

"You sonofa—What are you doing!" Panic sharpened her voice. Adrenaline spiked her pulse. Fear squeezed her chest.

He'd hit her intentionally. Even as the thought crystallized in her mind, the truck bashed into her again.

Sweat slickened her palms, and she pumped her brakes. The truck shot ahead of her when she slowed, and she breathed a sigh of relief. "Jerk."

But when she rounded the next curve, he was waiting for her. A chill streaked through her when she realized he was targeting her, not just randomly bullying. The truck's tires flung dirt and gravel from the side of the road as the driver wheeled back onto the highway. Neither speeding up or slowing to a crawl would shake him.

Finally, with trembling hands, she fumbled her cell phone out of her purse and dialed 911. Keeping the small phone between her cheek and shoulder was a challenge, but she wanted to keep both hands on the steering wheel. Ugh. Why hadn't she turned the phone back on the speaker setting before she left the hospital?

When the operator answered, Elise gave her name and approximate mile mark on the highway. "There's a truck, a silver quad-cab, and he's trying to run me off the road!"

Wham! The truck struck again. Hard. Her head snapped forward then back.

Elise dropped the phone as she fought to keep her car from careening off into the ditch. She muttered an unladylike curse that fit the situation. The cell phone lay on the floor of the passenger's side out of her reach.

Ahead, another sharp curve loomed, and signs proclaimed the approaching turnoff for Claiborne Lake. Her heart thundered.

Could she take the turnoff and lose the truck? She did a quick mental calculation. If she stopped on a side road, what would the guy do to her? She needed to find a populated place where she could have the protection and deterrent of witnesses. Just past the turnoff to Claiborne Lake State Park, a narrow two-lane bridge spanned the lake.

Surely, this maniac wouldn't keep up his game of chicken where they had no margin for error?

Nausea churned her gut. She had no such assurance. The driver was dangerous and completely unpredictable. Seeing the side road to the state park, Elise slowed to make the turn, but the truck slowed with her then pulled behind her.

He's preparing to follow if I turn, she thought.

But she was wrong. When she reached the road to the state park, the truck rammed her from behind, shoving her past the turnoff and into the scrubby weeds at the side of the road. Pulse racing and sour fear climbing her throat, Elise pulled back onto the road, determined to survive the madman's attack until she reached some sign of civilization and help.

But the truck driver had other ideas. As they approached the bridge over Claiborne Lake, he plowed into her back left fender, causing her front end to veer to the right. Off the road. Straight toward the embankment at the edge of the lake. Elise screamed when his intent became clear. He wanted her car to skid into the lake.

A jarring thump from behind. A free fall that made her stomach rise to her throat. And he'd achieved his goal.

Chapter 7

The nose of her car smacked the water, triggering her air bags and sending a jolt to her marrow. Elise's seat belt jerked taut across her chest with a bruising force. Her camera bag and purse flew forward onto the floor.

Once at rest in the lake, the car began sinking into the water, the weight of the engine pulling the hood down first. Elise coughed, choking on the powder released by the air bag. Stunned by the crash, she stared in disbelief as brown water crept toward her windshield. But as the initial shock faded and the reality of the danger she was in penetrated her fog, she rallied, flying into action. She had only seconds to get out of the car before it was submerged. Already the water level had reached her door, and the external pressure against the door was too great to open it. If she couldn't get out through the window soon, she'd be trapped. But the water had already shorted the car's electric wiring. The window wouldn't budge.

Jerking off her seat belt, she fumbled in her map pocket for the glass-busting hammer she kept there for just this type emergency. Before breaking her window, she grabbed her camera bag, purse and phone from the passenger-side floor. After zipping her cell in the waterproof camera bag and looping the straps around her neck, she took a deep breath for courage. She shielded her face from the window and gave the safety glass a firm whack with the spiked end of the hammer.

Shards of glass rained down and lake water, now at the base of her window, spilled into her car. Shoving the deflated air bag out of her way, she scrambled to hoist herself through the broken window. The jagged edges of broken glass sliced her hands as she fought her way out of the car. The chilly water soaked her clothes and stole her breath.

The car had landed only a dozen or so yards from the bank, and she began swimming in that direction as quickly as she could. The weight of her camera and purse dragged at her, and if she'd had farther to swim, she'd have ditched them rather than risk overtaxing herself before she reached shore. But her camera was her livelihood, and she wouldn't give it up if she didn't have to.

Finally after what felt like an eternity, she dragged herself up on the muddy bank and collapsed, panting. With trembling hands, she fumbled the zipper of the front pocket on her camera bag open and fished out her phone. *Please work!*

The screen lit when she opened it. Yes! Thank goodness for her waterproof camera bag. She prayed her camera had survived in good shape, too.

The crunch of footsteps in the dry leaves and gravel of the lakeshore roused her, and she glanced up to see who was coming. Sunlight backlit the man who approached, making it difficult to see his face.

But the large stick in his hand was clear enough. As was the pickup truck parked at the top of the embankment.

Panic swelled in her chest. A fresh surge of fear shot adrenaline to her limbs. She shoved to her knees just in time to see him swing the branch toward her in an arc. Elise gasped and raised her arms to protect her face, but the hefty stick cracked against her temple.

"Night, night," the man said as she slumped to the ground. And the world faded to black.

After leaving another message on Elise's voice mail, Jared tossed his cell phone on his kitchen counter and frowned. Where was she? What was taking so long?

"I knew I should have gone with her," he muttered aloud.

"Da-dee?"

He raised his gaze to Isabel who wore a liberal coating of applesauce on her hands and face. So much for letting her feed herself. Had she gotten *any* of the food in her mouth?

"Whatcha need, princess?" Jared grabbed a rag from a drawer to wipe her mouth before joining her at the kitchen table.

"Da-dee?" she repeated, holding a bite of her hot dog out to him in her grubby hand.

The innocent offering stirred warmth in his chest, and he smiled at her as he swiped at her dirty cheeks. "No, thanks, Izzy. I'll eat later. You finish your dinner."

Isabel popped the hot dog into her mouth and chewed, looking like a greedy chipmunk with full cheeks.

On the counter, his phone buzzed, and he hurried over to answer it. *Elise,* his caller ID read, and he released a relieved sigh.

"Thank goodness. I was getting worried. What was the hold up?" he said by way of greeting.

"Jared…" Her voice warbled, and if he had to guess, he'd say she was crying.

His stomach pitched, and his fingers tightened around the phone. "Elise? What's wrong? What did you find out?"

"Someone f-followed me. R-ran me off the road."

Static crackled over the line, while his nerves jangled with alarm. "What? Where are you? Are you all right?"

"I guess. I may…c-concussion… hit me over the—"

"Elise, you're breaking up. Say that again. Did someone hit you?" Jared paced closer to the window hoping to get better reception, even though he knew the bad connection was likely on her end.

"Car's in the wa—" More static. "Stole my c—"

An icy ball of fear lodged in his gut. He might not know the specifics, but enough frightening words had seeped through the static to tell him Elise was in trouble, possibly even in danger. He flew into action, grabbing his car keys and jacket, even before he knew where he was going or what he was doing. He only knew Elise needed help, and every protective instinct in him shouted for him to rush to her rescue.

"…to call the police. He might come b—"

"Elise, where are you?" He glanced to Isabel and realized he couldn't take her with him. Not if there was even a remote chance of danger. He began calculating where he could leave Izzy as he did a quick wipe of her mouth and fumbled one-handed to unfasten the safety strap in her highchair. Michelle was still sick…

"Stranded…bridge over Claiborne L—"

Lake, he finished mentally. He pictured the highway to Pine Mill and remembered crossing Claiborne Lake about ten miles south of Lagniappe.

"I'm coming. I have to drop Isabel at my parents' on my way out, but I'll be there as soon as I can. Okay?"

"Hurry," she said, and the static couldn't mask the tears in her voice.

He scooped Isabel up and grabbed the diaper bag by the door as he rushed to his car.

Concussion. Stole. Stranded. The words taunted him, painting horrific scenarios in his mind as he backed out of his driveway.

Dear God, please let her be all right. He couldn't bear losing another woman he cared about.

The sound of a car engine and tires on gravel brought Elise's head up from where she huddled, shivering on the lakeshore. A sheriff's deputy stepped out of his cruiser and started down the hill toward her.

Relief whooshed from her in a heavy exhale.

"They're here," she told the 911 operator who'd insisted she stay on the line until the police arrived. She thumbed off her phone and struggled to her feet as the deputy climbed down the embankment from the road.

Although she was glad to see any help at this point, she really wished Jared was the one pulling off the highway to her rescue. She longed for his arms to hold her and for him to murmur soft reassurances that she was safe. She'd called him as soon as she came to from the blow to her head that had knocked her out. She'd shoved aside the nagging questions about what it meant that he was the person she'd turned to, the one she'd wanted most at her time of need. If she were growing too attached to him, counting on him too heavily, she could deal with the repercussions later. Right now, she needed his strength, warmth and friendship. The peace and security she felt when she was around him.

"Are you all right, ma'am?" the deputy called, eyeing her bleeding temple then the car in the water.

"Define *all right*. I'm alive and mostly unhurt, but I've got a goose egg on my head, my car's taking a swim and my camera has been stolen."

The shudder that rippled through her this time had less to do with her damp clothes than the reminder of having come to with a throbbing headache, only to find her camera missing. Not her purse or phone. Just her camera. Which told her plenty. The man who'd knocked her out hadn't been interested in robbing her. He'd run her off the road in order to get the camera. Or more specifically the pictures on the camera. From the hospital.

What had she photographed that he didn't want her to see or have evidence of? Whose feathers had she ruffled with her photo session and interviews?

"Did you hit your head when the car crashed?" he said, pulling off his sunglasses and gently probing her wound.

"No, the guy who ran me off the road clobbered me with a big branch."

The officer arched an eyebrow. "Pardon?"

Elise launched into the full story of what had happened. She was telling the deputy about waking up to discover her camera missing, when a second car pulled off the highway. She shielded her eyes from the sun and gazed up the embankment.

"Elise!" Jared called, hastily descending the steep slope at the side of the road.

She staggered past the deputy and flung herself into Jared's open embrace. "Oh, Jared, I was so scared."

Concern dented his brow. "You're bleeding."

"Could have been much worse." She pointed to her car, the front end completely submerged. Jared's face drained of color, and she knew he was thinking of the way Kelly died. "But you're here, and except for a headache, I'm okay. That's all that matters." She curled her fingers in his jacket and pulled him close. "Just hold me for a minute, and I'll be fine."

He wrapped a firm hug around her, strong and possessive. Protective. "Jeez, Elise, you have no idea the scenarios I was imagining driving out here. I only caught bits of what you were saying when you called, and—"

Tucked in his arms as she was, she felt the shudder that rolled through him, the hammering beat of his heart.

"Ma'am," the deputy said, "I need you to sign this accident report with your statement. Dispatch tells me an ambulance is less than five minutes away. They'll check your head wound."

"I don't need—" she started, shaking her head, and the pain that ricocheted through her skull silenced her argument. She raised a hand to the bump on her head. "Ow. Okay, you win."

She pulled reluctantly from Jared's arms and scribbled her signature on the bottom of the accident report.

"We'll let you know if we learn anything about the guy responsible." The deputy tapped his hat in parting and trudged back up the hill to his cruiser as the ambulance arrived.

"Hit-and-run?" Jared asked.

"Literally." She pointed to her head.

His eyes widened, and his jaw tensed. "You were assaulted?"

"And my camera was stolen. I think my questions at Pine Mill Hospital this afternoon rattled someone's cage."

"You think you were targeted? Why?" He held up a hand. "Wait. Tell me once we get you out of here."

He put a hand under her elbow and helped her up the hill to meet the EMTs. Good thing, too, because her legs were still a bit rubbery. She declined the ambulance transport, promising Jared he could take her to the E.R. instead.

Once they were on the road, she laid out the events of the whole day. "At first, everyone was excited to have an article written about the hospital. I got the chance to take pictures and even be present at a birth with none other than Dr. Arrimand delivering."

"Isn't he the guy who delivered Grace?"

"Yeah, and get this—he also delivers babies at two other small hospitals in the area."

Jared jerked his gaze from the road to her. "Including the hospital where Kim Harrison delivered?"

"Ding, ding, ding. Give that man a prize. Yep, Crestview General where the Harrisons went, and Clairmont Community Hospital."

He returned his attention to the road and furrowed his brow. "Interesting."

"Dr. Arrimand was on duty while I was there. He was somewhat charming and friendly at first, and he granted me an interview, until…"

Jared arched an eyebrow. "Yeah?"

"His head nurse came in and whispered something to him. Then his mood changed dramatically. When I asked about the hospital's limited resources, specifically the critical-care facilities for newborns, he turned things around and began quizzing me on why I picked Pine Mill for my article and my past experience with the hospital. He became more and more closed off, and after Dr. Galloway brought me the reports he'd copied, Dr. Arrimand shut down completely."

"Who is Galloway?"

"The coroner. I learned some fascinating things from him, too, but the shift in Arrimand's behavior was what set off alarms for me. When Dr. Galloway left, Arrimand asked me to leave. When I asked about rescheduling to finish the interview, he refused."

"Sounds like he has something to hide."

"That's what I was thinking. And the mood change happened right after the nurse came in. What did she tell him?" she asked rhetorically as she stared out the window. "Then, as I was driving home, I was run off the road, and my camera was stolen."

Jared groaned, and his shoulders sagged. "So the thief has all the pictures you took at the hospital."

"Not exactly." She fished in her pocket and pulled out the memory card she'd taken from her camera earlier. "I have this."

Jared twitched a grin. "You're good."

"Well, it wasn't as much forethought or cunning as that the card was full, and I changed it. It doesn't have all the photos I took, but it has most of them." She took a deep breath and blew it out slowly. "What do you say we stick this baby in your computer and see what we've got? "

"After you get checked out at the E.R.," he said. "I would love to see if we can figure out what has the good doctor and his staff so worried."

Chapter 8

"You heard the doctor. You need someone to stay with you for a couple days," Jared argued as he helped Elise back to his car after she was released from the E.R. in Lagniappe. The hit to her head had caused a minor concussion, and someone needed to monitor her in case she experienced any side effects. "Because of Izzy, it's not practical for me to stay at your place. So you're coming to my house. Case closed."

"Jared, you don't have to—"

He stopped walking and caught her shoulders so that he had her full attention. "I want to. I need to be sure you're safe. I think it's obvious you riled someone with your questions, and they targeted you. I don't want them to have a second chance to hurt you."

Her face paled, and he pulled her into a tight hug.

"Do you have any idea how scared I was as I drove out to find you?" he murmured into her hair. After her swim in Claiborne Lake, she smelled slightly of fish and mud, but he didn't care. She was safe and relatively unharmed. "The thought of anything happening to another woman I cared about just—"

She tensed and lifted a querying gaze.

"What?" He traced her lips with a fingertip. "It surprises you that I care what happens to you? That you've become important to me?"

She ducked her head and leaned into him again. "I…I just— It's all just kind of overwhelming. Everything that's happened these last few weeks has my head spinning."

"You sure that's not the concussion?" He kissed her nose and gave her a half grin.

She groaned and closed her eyes. "I wish the painkillers they gave me would kick in. My head is throbbing."

A van pulled into the E.R. parking lot, and he guided Elise out of the van's path and to his car. "I don't mean to scare you, but you have to consider the possibility that whoever attacked you on the road might try to hurt you again."

She angled a dark frown at him as he unlocked the passenger door. "Yeah, it occurred to me."

"And what do you think they'll do when they realize they don't have the memory card from your camera?" She inhaled sharply and wavered on her feet. Drawing her back into his arms again, he rubbed her back. "They went to this much trouble to steal the camera. Do you really think they'll just give up?"

She shuddered, and he squeezed her tighter, wishing he could absorb her fear and shield her from any more pain. But ignoring the truth of her situation didn't serve any good. She needed to stay alert, take extra precautions, not turn a blind eye to possible trouble.

Elise tipped her head back to peer up at him. "I need

to tell MysteryMom what happened. I should send her the pictures I took, too."

"You can use my computer."

"No. If I'm going to stay with you, I need to stop by my place and pick up a few things. I'll bring my laptop."

Nodding, he opened the car door for her, and she slid carefully onto the seat. Elise directed him to her house but rode most of the way with her head leaned back and her eyes pinched closed in pain. At her house, he helped her to the door and took the keys from her when she fumbled them.

He unlocked her door, then stood back to let her enter first. A couple steps inside, Elise gasped and stopped so abruptly he nearly collided with her. "Elise? What—?"

Then he saw it. Her living room was in shambles, her possessions tossed from shelves and drawers, her sofa cushions upended. A cool draft drew his attention to the back door, which stood ajar.

"Oh, God. Someone's been here," she rasped.

She wobbled, and Jared quickly put an arm around her to steady her. "It looks like they were searching for something."

Her fingers clutched his wrist. "The memory card."

She was starting to hyperventilate, and he guided her toward a chair to sit down. "Breathe, sweetheart. Slow, deep breaths. I don't need you passing out on me."

"What if—"

A thump from the back of her house interrupted her, and they both tensed.

"They're still here!" she whispered, panic flooding her face.

"Stay here!" His tone brooked no resistance. Jared edged toward the hall, moving quietly. At the corner of the living room, he flattened himself against her wall out of sight and peered down the hall.

Another rustle drifted up the corridor. A shadow crept over the carpet. Jared tensed, adrenaline sharpening his senses.

Then a man in a gray fleece jacket stepped out of a back room, carrying her laptop. The intruder glanced warily down the hall then hustled toward Jared. Seeing no weapon in the burglar's hands, Jared swung out to block the man's escape. "Who are you? What are you doing here?"

Startled, the intruder halted. Briefly. Then he bared his teeth in a snarl and charged. He rammed Jared like a line-backer, his shoulder lowered to smash into Jared's chest.

Air whooshed from Jared's lungs, and he staggered back a step. Quickly finding his balance, Jared lurched for the intruder as the man tried to shove past him. With a wres-tler's hold, Jared tackled the thief and used his weight to send the man to the floor. As they fell, Elise screamed, and Jared prayed she stayed back, out of harm's way.

He pinned the man down, grappling with him for the upper hand. In the struggle, Elise's laptop came loose from the intruder's grip, and Jared knocked the computer out of reach.

With his hands relieved of the laptop, however, the in-truder was able to free a trapped arm. Before Jared could size up the threat, the man reared his arm back and landed a fist in Jared's jaw.

Jared had always thought the notion of seeing stars was hyperbole, but the pain that reverberated in his skull had him rethinking his belief. While he was dazed, the thief wrenched free and staggered to his feet. Jared scrambled to grab him. He managed to snag the bottom of the man's jacket, but the burglar shed the coat and darted out the back door.

"Jared!" Elise was at his side in an instant, gently probing his jaw with her fingers. "Are you all right? Your mouth
is bleeding."

He dabbed at his busted lip and slowly moved his lower
jaw side to side. "I'll live."

He rose to his feet, then helped her off the floor. "Call
the cops. I have his jacket, and they can probably get DNA
off it. And his fingerprints are going to be all over your
laptop."

She shook her head. "He was wearing gloves."

"He was?" He tried to picture what he'd seen as he battled the intruder but had to admit he'd been preoccupied,
trying to subdue the man.

She pulled her cell phone from her pocket and dialed.
"Latex, like they wear at the doctor's office."

His gut clenched. "Or the hospital."

She met his gaze, acknowledging his comment with a
troubled look, then turned her attention to answering the
911 operator's questions.

Jared dropped the jacket on a chair and went into the
kitchen in search of ice and a towel for his jaw. As he
assembled his ice pack, one thought played front and center
in his mind. What would have happened to Elise if she'd
come home to the intruder alone?

Somehow, Elise had poked a hornets' nest, and he feared
the worst was yet to come.

After Jared finished answering the police officers' questions, he went in search of Elise, who'd finished her interview earlier and disappeared to the back of the house.

He followed Elise's voice to the back room and found
her on her hands and knees, head down, bottom up, cooing
to something under the bed. "Come on, baby. That bad
man isn't going to get you. Come on, Brookie Wookie."

Brookie Wookie? Jared smiled to himself then tipped his head to admire the view of Elise's shapely fanny. When Kelly had gotten down on all fours like that to look under a bed or couch, he would give her a playful smack on the butt.

While Elise's derriere was a tempting target, he decided their relationship was not in a place he could take such intimate liberties, even in jest. But damn, she had a nice figure…

"That's a good girl," she said, backing up and pulling a tan-and-black tabby cat out from under the bed. She scratched the cat behind the ears and, hugging it close to her chest, kissed the tabby on the top of the head.

Jared pushed away from the door frame where he'd leaned his shoulder to watch and crouched beside Elise. He patted the cat's back. "Who's this?"

"Brooke. Can she come to your house, too? I don't want to leave her here alone."

"Sure." He flashed her a lopsided grin. "The more the merrier."

"Really?" She scrunched her nose skeptically. "You think your cats will mind?"

He grunted and scratched his chin. "Well, Diva will probably mind. She's earned her name. But she doesn't pay the mortgage. I do, and I say Brooke is welcome."

He put a hand under Elise's elbow and helped her to her feet while she cradled Brooke against her chest. On the bed, she'd already started filling a small travel bag with clothes and toiletries.

"I'll just go put her in her travel carrier," she said and headed out of the room.

Jared turned slowly, taking in the feminine decor, the personal touches that were uniquely Elise. Stepping over to her dresser, he studied an aged framed picture of a woman with two small children, a boy and a girl. Elise and her brother with their mother?

Next to the photo was a well-worn stuffed teddy bear with a ragged red ribbon around its neck, various bottles of lotion, perfume and nail polish, and a jewelry box, with its contents spilling out. His gut tightened. Had the intruder rifled through the box? It sickened him, infuriated him to think of the thug invading Elise's personal space, touching her private property, her most cherished possessions. If the intrusion bothered him this much, how must she feel?

He faced her bed and stared at the rumpled covers, picturing her lithe body wrapped in the silky sheets. Something pink and lacy peeked out from under her pillow. Heat flashed through him so hard and fast it stole his breath. He summoned the memory of the kiss they'd shared in the corridor outside the support-group meeting. Her lips had been warm and willing, sweet and soft. Desire coiled in his belly, and he gritted his teeth.

Cool it, Coleman. She's not looking for that kind of relationship. In fact, if what she'd told him the other night was true, she wasn't looking for any kind of relationship beyond friendship.

Huffing his frustration, he shifted his attention to her desk where drawers stood open with papers strewn about. Another spike of protective fury pumped through his blood. Nausea swamped him knowing the intruder had searched the space where Elise was at her most vulnerable, the room where she slept, where she let her guard down, where her secrets and heartaches should have been safe.

"Okay, we're ready." Her voice jolted him out of his musing. "Will you grab the bag on the bed?" She stood at the door with a pet carrier in her arms.

Brooke gave a plaintive meow from inside the cage.

Jared zipped her travel bag closed and hoisted it from the bed. He read her hesitation in her expression. "It's for the best, Elise. Especially now." *Now that someone has tried to kill you and has broken into your home.* The hollow, frightened look in her eyes told him the unspoken definition of *now* was understood.

He stepped closer to her and stroked a hand along her jaw, then cupped her cheek. "Elise, anyone trying to hurt you will have to come through me to get to you." He pressed a soft kiss on her lips and whispered, "I promise I will keep you safe."

"I'm afraid I didn't make a very good impression on your mother," Elise said, dropping wearily on the living-room sofa after she'd showered and changed clothes at Jared's house. "Coming in smelling like lake water and so rattled by the break-in, I could barely remember my own cat's name."

"Actually, she said she thought you seemed nice. Oh, and my brother and sister-in-law have invited you to come with me to their house next week for dinner." Jared handed her a mug of hot chocolate and sat down beside her. "The family is curious about the new lady in my life."

Isabel sat on the floor with a brightly colored set of rings that she fumbled to stack on a plastic post. Elise smiled when Isabel dropped a ring in place then clapped her hands, pleased with herself.

"Hey, good girl!" Jared cooed. He slid an arm around Elise's shoulders and tugged her closer. "There's a chicken casserole in the oven if you're hungry."

Elise shook her head. "No thanks." While sipping her cocoa, she spied Jared's orange cat sitting on the window-sill and asked, "Where are the other cats? They're getting along?"

"Well, Bubba didn't seem to mind having a visitor, but Diva is in a snit. She hissed and chased Brooke under my bed. I shut Diva in the laundry room, but Brooke has yet to come out."

Hearing his name, Bubba hopped down from the window and strolled over to the sofa. He sniffed Elise's feet then rubbed against her leg.

Isabel watched Elise bend over to scratch Bubba behind the ear. She squealed and pointed at Bubba. "Tee-tee."

Elise grinned. "Yeah, nice kitty."

"You speak baby? I'm impressed."

"Just one of my many talents," she said setting her hot chocolate on the coffee table. Tucking her bare feet beneath her, she leaned against the solid and reassuring warmth of Jared's chest.

"How's your head?" Jared strummed his fingers along her upper arm in hypnotizing strokes.

"The painkiller has kicked in and the hot shower helped relax me, so…I'm actually feeling okay right now."

He kissed her hair. "Good, 'cause I'm guessing tomorrow your muscles are gonna ache like the devil."

She groaned. "Probably."

"Ready to look at the pictures you took? Try to figure out what the thief didn't want you to see?"

Elise sighed and burrowed closer to Jared's warmth. "Not yet. I'm too comfy right now." She curled her fingers against his chest and pressed her ear over the steady thump of his heart. "After everything that's happened today, I just want to savor the quiet."

Isabel chose that moment to loose a high-pitched squeal of delight and bang the colored ring in her hand against the coffee table.

Jared chuckled, and Elise felt his laughter as a rumble

beneath her cheek. "What were you saying about the quiet?"

"Forget it. Quiet is overrated. I have too much of it at my house."

She watched Isabel inch her way wobbly step by wobbly step to the end of the coffee table then drop to her diapered bottom. Her target was clear as she started crawling toward Bubba. "Tee-tee."

A smile tugged Elise's lips, and she realized that the more she was around Isabel, the more she could appreciate, even cherish, the little girl's sweet innocence without a barrage of grief and regret over losing Grace. Was that because MysteryMom had instilled a hope in her that Grace was alive or because she was beginning to care for Isabel?

And what about her feelings for Jared? He'd been the only person she wanted beside her after her car had been run off the road into the lake. He was the one person who'd stood by her as she pursued MysteryMom's allegations. And in his arms was the only place she wanted to be at that moment. Cuddled with him, she felt safe after a perilous day, hopeful after the bleakest year of her life, and tempted to act on the attraction that smoldered between them. She was ready to put past romantic and family betrayals behind her and trust Jared with her heart.

"Well," he said, lifting her chin so that he could see her face, "you're welcome to come share the racket over here any time." He punctuated the invitation with a soft kiss.

Tendrils of desire unfurled deep inside her. Stretching closer to him, she deepened the kiss and sighed blissfully when he traced the seam of her lips with his tongue.

He whispered her name and tunneled his fingers into her hair to cradle her head between his palms. His kiss tasted like the creamy hot chocolate he'd been sipping, and she indulged in the sweetness of his lips on hers. Wrapping her arms around his neck, she wound her fingers in the hair at his nape and let her tongue tango with his.

He answered with a low growl of pleasure and eased her back on the sofa cushions. He followed her down, pinning her with his weight and the width of his shoulders. Rather than feeling trapped, she welcomed his embrace and the sense of shelter and protection his body provided.

She clung to him as he angled his mouth, his lips drawing deeply on hers and filling her with a growing hunger. With his taut muscles and hard angles pressed against her from head to toe, all her nerve endings were tingling and sparking, her body humming with tantalizing promise.

He smoothed a hand from her shoulder, over her breast and along her hip, his touch blazing a trail of fiery sensation. His caress held her so enraptured that she didn't notice the new presence by her head at first.

"Da-dee?"

Jared seemed not to hear the soft voice, but Elise angled her gaze toward the angelic blue eyes and slobbery grin at her eye level.

"Don't look now, but we have company," she said as he nuzzled her ear and covered the curve of her neck with nibbling kisses.

He continued nipping at her chin with toe-curling finesse and murmured, "Don't worry. She doesn't bite."

Elise chuckled and pushed against his chest. "Just the same, maybe we should put this on hold until after she's in bed."

He raised his head and gave Elise, then Isabel, considering looks. Arching an eyebrow, he sent his daughter a mock scowl. "Thanks for killing the mood, princess."

Rising to a seated position, he offered Elise a hand up, then smacked one last kiss on her lips before shoving to his feet. He scooped Isabel under the arms, tossing her a few inches into the air and catching her as she burst into fits of giggles and happy squeals. "Come on, priss, bath-time for you."

The father-daughter bond brought a smile to Elise's face, and a tender ache swelled in her chest.

Jared paused by the door to the hall. "If you're ready to start going through your pictures, I'll meet you at the computer as soon as I finish giving Isabel her bath."

Dragging herself off the couch, she crossed to the chair where she'd left her purse and dug the memory card out. "I guess I'm as ready as I'll ever be."

At Jared's computer, she inserted the program disk that would load her photo software, slid the memory card in the drive and began reviewing the shots she'd taken at the hospital. She scrolled through the images from radiology and the E.R. until she found the first pictures of the nursing staff at the maternity desk. Carefully she studied each face and the miscellaneous scenes she'd captured in the background of the shots. She searched for anything that she considered suspicious or worthy of the apparent concern she'd caused with her visit. She lingered over the photos of Dillon Thompson's birth, focusing more on what the doctor and nurse were doing than on the baby or parents. Frustration crept over her. Nothing seemed out of line. The birthing procedure followed the same regimen that she'd been through.

Except that Dillon's mother hadn't been drugged and put to sleep for the next several hours. And Dillon Thompson had been surrounded by family and friends in the hours following his birth.

The same twinge of envy that had poked her at the hospital needled her again. Would things have been different for her and Grace if she'd had a husband and parents, siblings and nephews all gathered in the hospital to welcome Grace to the world? To watch over her while Elise slept off the sedative?

Several minutes later, she heard the click of a door closing softly down the hall, and Jared entered the office with the baby monitor in his hand. "So have you come up with anything? What do the pictures show?"

"Nothing that stands out to me." She waved a hand toward the screen. "You're welcome to look, though. Maybe I'm missing something." She scooted out of the desk chair, and as Jared slid past her to take the seat, he caught her around the waist and planted a deep kiss on her mouth.

"Have I mentioned lately how glad I am that you're all right?" He brushed her cheek with his knuckles and searched her eyes with a hot, penetrating stare. Desire danced in the dark depths of his gaze, but she saw fear, as well.

Today, she'd revisited her nightmare by going to the hospital, the delivery room where she'd had—and lost—Grace. But Jared had also revisited the darkest day of his life when he'd heard she'd been in a car wreck. She knew his protectiveness, his insistence that she stay with him, had roots in that fear, in the memories of Kelly's tragic death.

"You have. And have I mentioned that I'm grateful for your help, so thankful that you were there for me today?" Elise wrapped her fingers around his hand and kissed his palm. The delicate scent that clung to his skin stirred a flurry of emotion in her chest. "Mmm, you smell good."

"Oh, yeah?"

"Yeah. Baby shampoo is one of the best smells in the world." She inhaled again, savoring the distinctive light scent. In the final days of her pregnancy, she'd stocked

Grace's nursery with baby shampoo and talc, lotions and washes. Following Grace's death, Elise had sat in the nursery, surrounded by the baby-fresh scents, and cried until her throat hurt. A bittersweet pang grabbed her, and she slipped away from Jared's arms to pace the floor.

Jared turned his attention to the computer screen and studied the pictures. "These are great pictures, Elise. Even if they don't show anything incriminating, your photo essay is going to be fantastic. You've captured such raw emotion on people's faces. Like this one, the little boy holding his arm against his chest."

She glanced over to see which shot he meant. "That was in the E.R. He'd broken it and was waiting to get a cast. He said what hurt most was knowing he couldn't play football again for a couple months."

"Well, you said you wanted to catalog all the stages and events of life that the hospital plays a part in. I'm sure this broken arm will stand out in that boy's memory the rest of his life." Jared clicked through a few more photographs and shook his head. Leaning back in the chair he linked his fingers behind his head. "Darned if I see anything worth running you off the road to steal your camera."

"You know, I keep going back to when the delivery-room nurse came in during my interview with Dr. Arrimand." Elise chewed her lip as she strolled across the floor and back restlessly.

Jared watched her from the computer chair. "You said earlier that was the turning point in his manner."

"He became stiff and suspicious and uncooperative, questioning me, clearly trying to get me to admit I'd been a patient. I figured it was pointless to deny the truth. He could have that information with a few keystokes anyway. Heck, that's probably what Nurse Ratched was telling him."

He grinned briefly at her movie reference, then furrowed his brow in thought. "Can you recall doing or saying anything to her that would have turned her against you?"

Elise shook her head. "On the contrary, she's the one who drugged me with the heavy sedative right after Grace was born."

"So…maybe whatever's happening over there…she's involved."

"A conspiracy?"

Jared turned a palm up. "I'd think there'd have to be a whole chain of people involved if records are going to be falsified, tracks covered, people deceived—"

Elise gasped. "The morgue records!"

Jared sat forward and shook his head. "What?"

"I started to tell you sooner but…remember I said Dr. Galloway came in and gave me some copies of the morgue's files?"

"And Arrimand clammed up completely after that and kicked you out?"

"Exactly. Dr. Galloway told me that only five newborn babies had been processed by the hospital morgue in the last two years." She explained everything that she'd discussed with the coroner and how his records proved that, if Grace had in fact died, there was no record to prove it. More evidence of the hospital's lies…or more specifically, Dr. Arrimand's and his head nurse's lies.

Jared gaped at her. "Where are those copies? I'd like to take a look."

She took a step toward the door. "I put them—" Elise felt the blood drain from her face, and a chill sweep through her. "Oh, my God." She pressed a shaking hand to her mouth. "I put them in my camera bag. Dr. Arrimand was right there. He saw me do it."

Jared shot out of his chair and closed the distance

between them. He steadied her with a hand on each arm. "Which means it might not have been your camera and pictures the thief was after at all, but the copies of the coroner's files."

"My proof that I was lied to about Grace, proof of a massive conspiracy." Elise drew a tremulous breath. "Proof that my daughter is alive."

Jared's grip tightened. "Dear God, Elise. If they know you're on to the scent of their conspiracy, whatever their game is, you're in more danger than you know."

Chapter 9

What were you doing at Pine Mill Hospital today?

Elise gaped at the message from MysteryMom that popped up in her instant-message window. No preamble, no greeting, no explanation of how she knew about Elise's trip.

She waved Jared over to the computer. "MysteryMom is online. Somehow she knows I was at Pine Mill today."

"How could she know that?" He settled beside her on a chair he'd brought in from the kitchen.

"I don't know," Elise said as she typed the same question for MysteryMom.

I just had a report from the agent who is undercover there. Your visit has really rattled some cages.

It has?

Yes. My agent found Dr. Arrimand and his nurse, Helen Sims, shredding documents and deleting files tonight. What were you thinking? I asked you to be patient and wait for me to report my progress to you. I asked you not to do any digging on your own that might cause suspicion.

Elise sat back in her chair, stung by MysteryMom's rebuke. Her fingers hovered over the keyboard for several seconds before she replied: I don't like being sidelined. I needed to do something.

No, you didn't. Your interference could blow a major investigation. We have several months and numerous resources invested, and before today, we were closing in on the evidence we needed to bring all the responsible parties to justice.

Acid filled Elise's stomach. What had she done?

More important, we were on track to trace what happened to the babies that were stolen and put up for adoption on the black market.

Black market. Elise froze when she read those words. The term *black market* conjured images of dangerous criminals and illegal weapons, espionage and dirty money. Could Grace have been a pawn in something so awful?

She glanced at Jared, whose face had lost some color as he read the instant messages with her.

"My baby was sold on the black market, Jared. My daughter!" She fought the hysteria that crept into her voice.

Jared wrapped his fingers around her wrist and gave her

a comforting squeeze. "You better tell her what happened to you, what you found out. She needs to know."

With a nod, Elise turned back to the keyboard. She explained everything to MysteryMom from the conception of her article and photo essay through finding the intruder searching her home.

MysteryMom made no reply for several minutes, long enough to make Elise worry. Finally, MysteryMom posted:

Do you have a friend you can stay with for a few days? I'm terribly afraid you've put yourself in the line of fire. Dangerous people could come after you again to silence you.

Icy tendrils of dread spread through her, and she shot Jared a horrified look.

He nudged her out of the way and typed, Yes, she can stay with me. I'll make sure she's safe.

Who are you?

Her boyfriend.

Elise caught her breath and raised a puzzled gaze to his.

"You have an objection to the term?" He tucked a wisp of her hair behind her ear.

Pleasant shivers chased through her from his touch. "I…don't know."

A muscle in his jaw twitched as he studied her, his eyes moving over her like a caress. "What would you call me? I think we both know we're more than friends." He leaned closer, brushing his lips against hers. "I'd like to be much more."

Heat suffused her blood as she imagined her naked body

twined with Jared's, the feel of his hands on her skin, his mouth exploring her most sensitive places.

"Jared…" she'd started when a new instant message popped onto the screen with a beep. She angled her head to read MysteryMom's reply.

Elise, you've been talking to other people about this?

Only Jared and my grief-support group. But everything we say there is in the strictest confidence.

In the delay before MysteryMom's reply, Elise could almost hear the other woman's groan and see her disappointed head shake.

Don't talk to anyone. If you want to be kept in the loop on our progress, it is essential that you follow my directions. With just one mistake, the whole operation could blow up in our face. I have people in precarious positions—dangerous positions if their cover is blown. We are so close to putting all the pieces together and dismantling the baby-selling ring.

A chill burrowed to her core. *A baby-selling ring.* She had thought Grace had been taken by a few warped individuals, but the scope of the evil that she'd fallen victim to shook her.

She typed, I'm sorry. I know that's probably too little, too late, but with my daughter's life on the line, I couldn't just sit on my hands. I had to *do* something.

I understand your restlessness. I'm a mother, too. But in my line of work, failure to follow orders can get you or one of your agents killed. It could be your life at risk if you don't back off and let us handle this. You've already made yourself a target with your questions today. These people have millions of dollars at stake. They won't take kindly to anyone disrupting their operation.

Elise shivered, and Jared slid onto her chair, pulling her onto his lap and wrapping her in his arms. She closed her eyes and soaked in the comforting strength and reassurance of his embrace, trying to absorb the magnitude of what was happening to her, what she'd unwittingly become a part of.

The beep of the IM drew her attention back to the screen.

I have to go now. I'll be in touch as soon as I have something to report. Stay safe and lie low. Okay?

Elise panicked. MysteryMom was her only link to Grace, and she was desperate for even the smallest piece of information about her.

Elise typed, Wait!

Yes?

Have you learned anything about Grace? Was she sold? Where she was sent? Who has her?

I don't know anything definite yet. We're getting close, but you must trust us.

Elise's stomach rolled. She wanted to tell MysteryMom how difficult it was for her to trust anyone. She'd already been betrayed by the people she should have been able to trust the most—her father, her lover, her doctor.

The icon beside MysteryMom's avatar disappeared, letting her know her secret advocate had logged off.

She continued to sit on Jared's lap, still and silent, absorbing everything she'd learned, everything that had happened. Having Jared's arms around her, his broad shoulder under her cheek, gave her a sense of security and stability when everything else in her life was shifting and shattering. He rubbed a warm hand up and down her back, comforting her the way she'd seen him calm Isabel. Tender. Loving.

"So what do you think?" she said finally.

He filled his lungs with a deep breath before answering. "I think you are lucky to be alive and… I'd like to keep you that way. I'll fix up the guest room for you."

"I mean, what do you think about there being a black market for selling babies? That's just so…mercenary and depraved." She gave an involuntary shudder, and he hugged her tighter, kissed her hair.

"Hence the term *black market*."

She hummed her agreement distractedly.

"As horrible as it is, there will always be those who prey on vulnerable people to make a buck. These black marketeers know that couples who can't have children of their own sometimes get impatient or desperate. Maybe they've been turned down for adoption, or get frustrated with the red tape. When we decided to adopt, we met couples that were to the point they'd have paid any price and broken any law if they thought it would get them the child they wanted."

"Even if they knew the child they were buying had been stolen from her mother?"

He massaged her neck, working the tense muscles. "It's been a long, stressful day for both of us, and a warm bed is sounding pretty good about now."

She nodded stiffly, knowing that despite the weary ache in her limbs and her recent lack of sleep, she'd likely lie awake most of the night rehashing the day's events.

When she made no move to get up, Jared handed her the nursery monitor. When she gave him a puzzled look, he slid an arm behind her knees and another across her back, then lifted her as he stood. Cradling her in his arms, he headed to the hallway where he stopped.

She curled her fingers in the fabric of his shirt. "Where are we going?"

"That's up to you." He met her gaze, awaiting a response, but she could see from his expression that he was asking more than just which room to carry her to. Her answer spoke for what she wanted from their relationship. Did she trust him enough to become his lover? Did she still need time and emotional distance to sort out her feelings for him? Was friendship all she could ever give him?

She stroked a hand along the evening's growth of stubble on his chin and murmured, "Your room."

Her answer obviously pleased him, but his grin wasn't cocky or smug. Just…happy. And when she considered it, her decision brought her contentment and joy, as well. She'd already trusted Jared with her darkest fears, her deepest pain, her most private anguish. Sharing a physical intimacy with him felt ordained, predestined.

Jared laid her on his bed, pausing only long enough to remove his shoes and belt before he stretched out beside her and propped his cheek on a bent arm. "Unfortunately, I'm…not prepared for this."

"Not prepared? I take it you were never a Boy Scout?"

"Actually I was for a few years, but…the thing is, I haven't been with anyone since Kelly died, and we never needed contraception because she couldn't conceive."

"I see. So no condoms in the house?"

He pulled a face. "Sorry. If you'll watch Izzy, I can run out and get—"

"Wait." Elise looped an arm around his neck as he rose and chuckled. "You didn't ask me if I was on the pill."

He arched an eyebrow. "Are you on the pill?"

"No."

He frowned.

"But I use something even better." She pushed the waist of the borrowed sweatpants low on her hip to reveal her birth-control patch.

His gaze heated, and he traced the patch, then lower with his finger. "Nice."

He bent his head to kiss the skin she'd exposed to him, and Elise threaded her fingers through his hair. The scratch of his beard so low on her hip sent shockwaves through her.

"I like a woman who plans ahead." He moved his kiss to her navel and nuzzled her belly.

"Not that I've had any real use for it recently, but it helps ease my cramps each month." She winced and bit her lip. "Uh-oh, TMI?"

He raised an amused grin. "Don't worry about it. After all the diapers I've changed and baby spit I've cleaned up, nothing really shocks me anymore." He stretched up to give her a quick kiss on the mouth before hooking his fingers in her sweatpants and dragging them down slowly. He blazed a path with his mouth, an inch at a time, as he exposed more of her flesh.

Elise grabbed handfuls of the bedspread as he coaxed the sweats down her thighs and nibbled his way toward her knees. When he finally worked the pants down her calves and off her feet, already bare from her shower, he massaged her toes and her instep with deep rubs of his thumbs.

A moan escaped her throat, and she closed her eyes to savor the exquisite pampering. She'd never known her feet could be an erogenous zone, but as his ministrations continued, her body grew relaxed, and her skin sensitized from head to toe. Every touch as he worked his way back up her legs, caressing and tasting, sent shimmering tingles of anticipation to her core.

Most of her life, she'd fought stubbornly for control, to protect her heart and maintain her independence. After her father had abandoned her and her brother to a foster home, she'd been determined not to give anyone the power to hurt her so deeply again. Yet surrendering her body to Jared felt as natural as breathing. She didn't question why she instinctively trusted him, why his touch felt so... right.

But indulging the desire that had been growing between them didn't mean she would lose her head—or her heart—to him. Mind-numbing sex at the end of a hellish day was her right. She refused to believe her comfort level with Jared meant anything more than mutual respect.

As his kiss grazed the juncture of her thighs, she sucked in a rough gasp, and all rationalizations fled her brain in a wave of heady lethargy.

He freed one button at a time on the flannel shirt he'd lent her, parting the soft fabric and feathering his tongue over the skin he revealed. A thrum of desire and need coiled inside her as his slow seduction continued. He undressed her at a leisurely pace and treated every part of her to a tender caress and warm kisses. When she was naked, his gaze traveled over her with every bit as much heat and possessiveness as his fingers.

"You're beautiful," he whispered, scooting across the mattress to align his body with hers.

"And you're wearing too many clothes," she replied, hooking her legs around his thighs and cupping his buttocks with her hands.

"Hmm," he hummed capturing her lips for a deep, sexy kiss. "What should we do about that?" He used his thumb to trace her collarbone, then slid lower to circle her breast. Her nipples peaked, anticipating his touch.

Eager to feel his skin against hers, she fisted his shirt in her hands and dragged it over his head. He tossed the T-shirt aside, and Elise pressed her body closer. The pleasure of her breasts grazing the coarse sprinkling of hair on his chest electrified her already-crackling synapses. Her hands explored his back, savoring the contrast of supple skin over taut muscle.

Insinuating her hand between them, she began fumbling with the fly of his jeans. After a moment, Jared rolled beside her and finished the task, whisking his jeans and briefs off in one efficient motion.

When he moved back toward her, she planted a hand on his chest to stop him. Leaning up, propped on one arm, she drank in the sight of his lean torso and masculine physique. "You're rather beautiful yourself."

He arched an eyebrow. "Beautiful?"

She flashed him a saucy grin and trailed a fingernail up his thigh to his belly. "In the most he-manly way, of course."

"I th—"

Whatever he'd intended to say was lost in a hiss of pleasure, as she wrapped her hand around his heat and stroked the length of him. With a playful growl, he rolled on top of her and seized her mouth with a scorching kiss. He tangled his tongue with hers and settled in the V of her legs.

Elise raised her hips, increasing the friction of his body against hers. The clambering need inside her flashed hotter. She hadn't been with a man in years, but nothing in her experience equaled the powerful sensations that coursed through her, building, hovering just beyond reach.

Jared moved his attention to her breasts, drawing each taut peak into his mouth in turn. With one hand, he reached between them to caress her intimately, sliding a finger inside her. She gasped and thrust her hips off the mattress, ready to fly apart at any moment. "Jared!"

He needed no further coaxing. With a bold, sure stroke, he buried himself inside her, filling her and sending her into a dizzying maelstrom of sensation.

He gave a ragged groan and tightened his hold on her as she shuddered and pulsed around him. She clung to him, a knot of emotion clogging her throat, stealing her breath. Elise squeezed her eyes shut and swallowed hard, determined to shove down the ache that reached into her heart, refusing to attach any foolish romantic notions to their intimacies. Jared had made her no promises, and she had no right to expect any commitments from him. Tonight was about savoring the moment. About escaping reality for a few precious minutes. About sex.

When her body quieted, he began a sensual withdrawal, followed by a deep return glide. Just when she thought she'd pinnacled, he showed her a greater pleasure, a higher plane of ecstasy. His rhythmic lovemaking carried her higher, until they soared together to an earthshaking climax.

He held her close, his breath warm against her neck in the aftermath of their passion. Their bodies cooled, and he pulled a quilt around them, creating a cocoon that allowed her to pretend for a few minutes longer that nothing existed beyond this moment, this man, this peaceful contentment.

But a whimpering cry crackled over the baby monitor

on the nightstand, and Jared jerked from sated lethargy to parental attention in a heartbeat. "Sorry. Duty calls."

She gave him a hard deep kiss. "Don't apologize. If you didn't jump to tend to her, I'd have to rethink my association with you."

He grinned and flipped back the quilt, letting a wave of cold air into her snuggly cave. She shivered and slid to the edge of the bed. "Want me to go? Will she let me rock her, you think?"

He pulled on his pants and glanced at her. "Feel free to give it a try."

Elise threw on her borrowed clothes again and, with Jared on her heels, hurried to Isabel's room. The baby girl stood at the side of her crib, clinging to the side rail, mewling sleepily. When she saw Elise, she held out her arms and whimpered, "Mee-mee."

Elise's heart stopped, her breath stuck in her lungs. "D-did she just call me Mommy?"

Jared nudged her aside to approach the crib. "Sounded a little like it, but Mimi is what she calls Michelle."

Elise stepped forward, feeling foolish for her assumption. Why would Isabel think of her as a mother figure when she'd only seen Elise a handful of times? She drew a deep restorative breath, warning herself, *Don't start painting fanciful family portraits of yourself with this man and his child just because you slept with him.*

She watched Jared stroke Isabel's soft curls and murmur reassurances to her, and her heart melted. Painful longing, not only for the child she'd lost, but the family life she wanted, wrenched in her chest.

He lifted Isabel from the crib and turned to Elise. "Want to try rocking her?"

She nodded, not trusting her voice not to crack. She reached for the baby, and Isabel tucked her head under

Elise's chin, snuggling against her chest with the blind
trust of the innocent. A melancholy mix of tenderness
and regret speared Elise's soul as she settled in the rocking chair and patted Isabel's back.

Diva trotted in from the hallway and gave a meow that
sounded surprisingly loud in the quiet of the dark nursery. By the glow of the nightlight, Elise spotted Bubba
and Brooke lurking restlessly in the hallway. "Looks like
everyone's up for a midnight snack."

Jared scooted Diva toward the hall door with his foot.
"You seem to have things under control in here, so I'll go
slop the hogs and...meet you back in bed in a few?"

The question mark in his tone told her he was as uncertain where they were headed with their relationship as
she was.

And he was leaving the direction they took up to her.
What did she want from him? Was she going to return to
his bed for the cuddling and intimacy of sleeping in his
arms? Or was she going to distance herself emotionally
by spending the remainder of the night in her guest bed?

Diva rubbed against Jared's leg and yowled again impatiently. Elise felt as if the cat were rushing her, pressing
her to examine her feelings for Jared, for Isabel, for her
future. When had everything in her life become so topsy-
turvy and confusing?

My sources tell me that your baby might be alive.

Yeah, that was the moment.

Elise pressed her cheek to the silky hair on Isabel's head,
inhaled the sweet fragrance of baby shampoo and angled
a glance toward Jared.

Jared was here and now. Real. Certain.

She grinned. "Yeah, I'll meet you in a few."

Chapter 10

An hour later, after making love to Jared again, Elise curled her body against his and trailed a finger down his chest. Settling her hand over the steady thump of his heart, she tipped her chin up to meet his gaze. "Will you tell me about how you adopted Isabel?"

"Sure." He brushed her hair back from her eyes. "What do you want to know?"

"Everything. Did you know her mother? Were you at her birth?"

He shook his head. "We don't know much about Isabel's mother, except that she was a teenager from Lake Charles who was eager to give her baby up for adoption so she could go back to being a teenager."

"So you've never met the girl?"

"No. On purpose. We used a 'boutique' adoption agency—" He drew quotation marks in the air with his fingers "—That specialized in closed adoptions. A friend of ours had heard about the agency through another couple that had used them."

"What made them a 'boutique' agency?" she asked, copying his finger quotations.

"You mean other than the exorbitant fees?" Jared remembered his shock when he'd first learned what the agency, Second Chance, charged for an adoption.

She tipped her head back to meet his eyes. "Their fees were higher than regular adoption agencies?"

"I'll say. Well, maybe not higher than international adoptions. I hear they can get pricey, too."

"So why pay it? What did you get for your higher fee?"

"Peace of mind, mostly. Most of the other agencies we talked to had some degree of openness to the adoption. A lot of the mothers wanted to be able to visit their child or leave the door open for the child to find them later if they wanted."

"You don't want Isabel to search for her biological mother when she's older?"

"Not necessarily. I guess I'll leave that up to Izzy when she's older."

"Then why the closed adoption?"

"Kelly was terrified that a few months after our adopting, the birth mother would change her mind and demand we return the baby. When we told people we were adopting, suddenly everyone had horror stories about couples losing their children to biological parents who'd had a change of heart."

Elise grunted. "Why do people do that? When I was pregnant with Grace, I was besieged with deliveries-gone-wrong stories and sick-or-preemie-baby stories." She sighed. "Little did I know I'd end up with my own nightmare to tell future mothers-to-be."

He squeezed her arm and pulled her closer for a kiss on

her head. "The same dark side of our human nature that makes people rubberneck at accident scenes, I guess."

"So how old was Isabel when you got her? Did you choose her or…did the mother choose you or…how did that work?"

"We drove down to Baton Rouge to pick her up when she was just two days old. We told the agency we didn't care what sex our baby was, so when she was born and brought to the agency's nursery, we were next on the list of approved couples waiting for a baby. We'd been on the list for about six months before we got the call." Jared grinned, remembering the day the call had come.

A kick of excitement spun through him, just as it had that day over a year ago when Second Chance had called. "We had only been up for a few minutes, and I was still making coffee. Kelly was in the shower. All I heard the woman say was 'we have a baby girl for you' and 'pick her up today.' We left the house so fast, Kelly's hair was still wet, my shirt was inside out, and we never drank the coffee I'd brewed. I'm lucky I didn't get a speeding ticket." He chuckled, and Elise angled a grin at him. "Although we joked about telling the cop we were having a baby if we were pulled over."

"That might have been a tough sell since Kelly wasn't pregnant."

"On the way home, though, I drove like a grandpa on a Sunday drive. I had precious cargo on board, and I wasn't about to run a yellow light or test the speed limits."

"I found myself driving slower and taking fewer chances in simple things when I was pregnant. I held the railing going down stairs, waited for longer breaks in traffic before crossing streets, and didn't develop any of my own film for fear the chemical fumes would hurt Grace."

She tugged her mouth in a lopsided grin and shook her head. "Silly, I know."

Jared combed his fingers through Elise's hair, gratified that she could smile when she shared memories of her pregnancy. "Not silly. It shows you care, and you were protecting your child."

Her eyebrows drew together in a scowl, and he knew immediately she was agonizing over her inability to protect Grace after her birth.

"You still use film in this digital age?" he asked to distract her.

"Sometimes. When I'm feeling artsy about my photography, I use film. I'll never give up my 35 mm if for no other reason than it was my first good camera as a kid. A gift from my mother. Sentimentality, you know."

"Absolutely. I still have my grandfather's slide rule he used for his engineering courses in college." He ruffled her hair a bit. "Don't know how to use it, but…"

She propped up on an elbow to gaze down at him with a speculative expression. "Why couldn't Kelly have children?"

"She had to have a hysterectomy when she was a kid. Her family was in a car accident, and her pelvis was crushed. She lost a kidney, too."

"Jeez. So she was in *two* major car accidents?"

"Mmm-hmm. One took her ability to have kids. One took her life." He twisted his mouth in thought. "I never heard her complain about her circumstances, though. She considered herself lucky to have survived that first accident, lucky her family survived. She focused on the positive. Always."

"She sounds like a remarkable woman."

"She was." His gaze dropped, and he added quietly,

"She was a good mother, too. She couldn't have loved Isabel more if she were her own flesh and blood."

Elise drew a hand along Jared's cheek, pulling his attention back to her. "So do you. I see it whenever you're with her."

He nodded, and a proud smile curved his lips. "She's my whole world. I don't know how I'd survive if anything happened to her." A second after he'd said it, he tensed, realizing how the comment sounded. "Jeez Louise, Elise," he said with a groan. "I did it again. I'm sorry. I can't seem to stop putting my foot in my mouth around you."

"And I thought I asked you to stop tiptoeing around me. I'm okay." She thought about MysteryMom's assurance that they were close to finding out what happened to Grace, and a smile ghosted across her lips. "Besides, I'm holding out hope that MysteryMom will help me get Grace back. Focus on the positive, right?"

He hugged her closer and kissed the crown of her head. "Right." Jared fell into a pensive silence then, staring up at the ceiling. When a frown puckered his brow, Elise propped herself on an elbow again.

"What? You look so serious."

He sighed. "I was just wondering..."

"Yeah?"

"About the people that might have Grace. If they bought a baby on the black market, they must have wanted a child pretty desperately. And...I'm guessing they've fallen in love with Grace as much as I have Isabel."

A chill slithered through Elise. She had purposely avoided thinking about the bond her baby might have made with some other woman and vice versa. Not that she didn't hope Grace had been well-loved and cared for, but because it created an ethical dilemma she hated to consider.

"How can I take Grace away from them if they're the only family she's ever known?"

"Exactly. I mean, I know she's your daughter, your flesh and blood, but…they've built their lives around her, formed bonds and—"

"We don't know that. I mean, I hope they have, but then I hope…Oh, God, Jared. What am I supposed to do? She's *my* daughter. I want her back."

"I know. I just…"

Elise shoved down the guilt that crept over her. "If they bought her on the black market, they have no legal right to her. I have every right to stake my claim to her and take her back." She clung to that precept, ruthlessly convincing herself she had nothing to feel guilty about. "I definitely want her back, and I'll hire a lawyer to do it if I have to."

Jared said nothing for a long time, and she could feel the tension and distance between them growing by the second because of her decision.

"That's what I thought you'd say." Regret hung heavy in his tone and, tossing aside the covers, he slid out of bed.

Elise sat up, holding the covers against her bare breasts. "Where are you going?"

He paused at the doorway, swiping a hand over his mouth as he sighed. "I, um…thought I'd check on Isabel."

But she saw his departure for what it was. An excuse. A need for distance. The first fissure in what could become a gulf that divided them. Would he really oppose her if she fought Grace's adoptive parents for custody? She'd believed she had his unflagging support and friendship. Which was stupid really. After all, hadn't her own father found it easy to cast her aside when she became an inconvenience? No relationship was unconditional.

And she'd be wise to remember that. Better that she reel

in the tender emotions toward him she toyed with tonight than in a few months find herself with another broken heart.

On Monday morning, Elise stared at the blinking cursor on her computer screen and replayed MysteryMom's warning not to do anything that could jeopardize the investigation her team had in progress. Surely that didn't include her photo essay and article on the circle of life at the small-town hospital. Her editor was waiting for her piece. This was her chance to prove herself valuable to the newspaper at a time when newspapers across the country were shrinking staffs.

"It doesn't work by telepathy."

Roused from her musing by the male voice, she turned and found Jack Calhoun, one of the newspaper's star reporters, sipping a mug of coffee behind her and grinning.

He aimed a finger at her keyboard. "See those buttons with letters on them? You have to push those to make the words appear."

She flashed him a lopsided grin. "Oh, is that how it works?"

He wiggled his eyebrows. "Amazing, huh?"

She rubbed the back of her neck. "Any tips on what order to push the keys? What words I should make appear?"

He snorted. "That's for you to figure out, greenhorn."

"You're so helpful," she called to him as he strolled away, then swiveled her chair toward her monitor. Flexing her fingers, she started pounding the keys, letting her creative juices flow. She wrote the article she'd envisioned, an eloquent depiction of a slice of life as witnessed by the small-town hospital. She kept her references to the labor-and-delivery and maternity wards as general as possible, focusing primarily on Dillon Thompson's birth and his parents' joy.

She was detailing the story of the boy with the broken arm in the emergency room when her cell phone chimed, alerting her that she had an email.

She fished the phone out of her purse and checked the screen.

I have new info. We need 2 talk. Can u log on msg board so we can IM? —MysteryMom

Elise's breath hung in her throat. Could MysteryMom have found Grace already? She replied, Logging on now, then quickly signed on to the newspaper internet connection.

MysteryMom was waiting for her at the Parents Without Children message board and sent an IM immediately. Elise leaned close to her monitor, her mouth dry with anticipation, and read.

My people have traced a few of the missing babies, including Grace, to an adoption agency called Second Chance. Not all of their adoptions are black market, which allows them to serve as a front for the illegal adoptions.

Tears stung her eyes. She was one monumental step closer to knowing what happened to her baby. With trembling hands she typed, Have you found Grace? Was she still at Second Chance?

No to both. We are trying to narrow down which family adopted her, but we aren't there yet. I'll keep you posted.

I don't know how to thank you. This means so much to me!

It's my pleasure. Remember, keep this close to the vest until the whole operation is complete and we bring these guys to justice.

I will.

Stay safe.

MysteryMom logged off, and Elise rocked back in her chair. A smile crept to her lips, and the warmth of hope spread through her.

Jared. She had to tell Jared the wonderful news. Snatching up her cell phone, she tapped the screen and called his number. She didn't stop to question why her natural impulse was to share her joy with him. He'd stood by her throughout the twists and turns of the past few weeks, and she wanted him beside her when she finally got Grace back. He'd believed in her and comforted her when she needed a friend, and that support meant the world to her.

Friend. The word stuck out as she listened to his phone ring. They'd been so much more than friends the last couple of nights. She'd slept in his arms, made love with him, whispered intimacies in the dark of night. Would she even want to go back to her own house when MysteryMom told her she was safe to return home? Had she already gotten in too deep with Jared? She prayed she hadn't set herself up for more heartache.

Jared hovered over a set of blueprints at a new construction site, consulting with one of his carpenters, when his cell phone buzzed.

He pulled it from the clip at his belt and thumbed the answer key without taking his eyes off the blueprint. "Jared Coleman."

"Hi, it's Elise. Sorry to bother you at work, but I have news."

He raised a finger to ask the carpenter to wait for a minute, then stepped away to talk in private. "Not a problem. In fact, I was going to call you later. Michelle wants us to eat dinner with them tonight. Are you game?"

"Tonight? I—"

"I know I told you it would be later in the week, but she's eager to get to know you. She figured out you stayed with me over the weekend, and she gave me the third degree."

"Really? What did you tell her?"

"Mostly to mind her own business. But I think my sappy grin gave me away." He smiled the way he had around his sister-in-law that morning. Smiling was easy when he recalled the incredible nights he'd spent with Elise and the lazy days they'd enjoyed, playing with Isabel and watching rented movies from his couch.

"I had a good time this weekend, too." He could hear the smile in her voice, and his chest filled with warmth.

"So I can tell her yes?"

"Sure. Sounds great."

He switched the phone to his other ear and leaned against a sawhorse. "You said you have news?"

"I do. I heard from MysteryMom this morning. She's tracked down the adoption agency that was selling the missing babies on the black market." Excitement filled her tone, and his own pulse picked up, catching her enthusiasm. "She said Grace is one of the babies that went to this agency."

Jared perked up, his grin widening. "That's great! Does that mean they know where Grace is now?"

"Not yet. Apparently the agency also handles legitimate adoptions as a cover so they can work the black-market ring on the side," she said. "The place is called Second Chance."

Jared jolted, nearly dropping the phone. Blood rushed past his ears in a deafening *whoosh,* and ice settled in his veins. Second Chance had sold black-market babies?

Acid pooled in his gut.

Isabel! Could Izzy be one of the stolen babies? Even the possibility left him cold and shaking to his core.

"I don't suppose you heard anything about Second Chance when you were looking into adopting Isabel, did you?"

"I—" Jared swallowed hard, panic swamping him. "No. I've…never heard of it." He winced as the lie tumbled off his tongue. Instantly he regretted the fib, but a gut-level protective instinct shouted down his conscience. Until he saw where this new information led, until he could reassure himself that Isabel's placement with him was safe, he had to proceed with caution.

"Oh, well. I just thought…whatever. Anyway, Mystery-Mom promised to let me know when she learned more, but…isn't it exciting? I'm so close to getting Grace back, Jared. I can feel it!"

He dragged in a rough breath and clenched his back teeth. *Cool it, Coleman. Don't overreact.* "Um, yeah. That's great. Listen, I have to go…"

"Of course. So I'll see you tonight? Dinner with Michelle and Peter?"

He wished he could get out of his promise to eat with his brother's family. He needed time to do his own investigating concerning Second Chance. Pinching the bridge of his nose, he said, "Yeah. See you tonight."

After disconnecting with Elise, Jared stared silently at

the dirt at his feet, stewing. He and Kelly had made inquiries about Second Chance before they adopted. They'd
seen the agency's state license, had the recommendation
from a friend who'd used them.

*Apparently the agency also handles legitimate adop-
tions as a cover...*

Nausea swamped him. Dear God, let Isabel's adoption
be one of the legal ones! If MysteryMom's people exposed
Second Chance in their operation to stop the black market
baby-selling ring, Isabel's adoption could prove to have
been illegal. Could charges be filed against him for his
part in an illegal adoption? He'd operated in good faith,
even if Second Chance might not have.

Or worst of all, a judge could demand he return Isabel.
The courts could take his daughter away.

The sick swirl of acid in his gut surged up his throat,
and he forced the bile back down by sheer force of will.

Don't get ahead of yourself. He had no evidence that
Isabel's adoption wouldn't stand, and he'd not give his
daughter up without a fight.

But he had no time to lose. MysteryMom's people were
digging into the files at Second Chance at that moment. He
had to gather his own facts and be ready to protect Isabel
from whatever storm might be coming.

"This chicken is delicious, Michelle. I really appreciate
your including me tonight," Elise said as she passed the
basket of rolls to Peter.

"Well, we're happy to have the chance to get to know
you better." Michelle smiled at her guest. "And it's a super
easy recipe. I can print out a copy for you if you want."

"I'd love that," Elise returned.

Jared scooted his food around his plate, only half listening to the niceties being bantered about the dinner table.

His appetite had been squelched by the alarming information Elise had given him earlier about Second Chance.

In her high chair, Isabel squeezed a handful of peas and giggled as they oozed through her fingers.

"I know we kinda bumped this dinner up in the week," Michelle said, "but we have some good news to share, and I couldn't sit on it any longer!"

Curious, Jared raised his head, turning his attention to Michelle. His sister-in-law's happy tone reminded him of the excitement he'd heard in Elise's voice that morning. He prayed Michelle's news didn't have the dark side for him that Elise's had.

"Turns out I didn't have a stomach virus last week. It was morning sickness." She paused, sending Peter a wide smile when he wrapped his hand around hers. "We're having a baby. I'm due in June."

From the corner of his eye, he saw Elise cast him a side glance. His brother and sister-in-law watched him, as well, waiting for his reaction. A dozen thoughts filtered through his brain in rapid succession. Joy for his brother. Concern for how Elise would feel about the talk of babies. Bittersweet reminders of receiving the news that Isabel was waiting for him and Kelly.

He glanced quickly to Isabel's messy face, and his heart twisted. Knowing an appropriate reply to Michelle's announcement was needed, he shook off the momentary shock, pasted on a smile and quipped, "Well, it's good to know you were listening when we had our talk about the birds and the bees in seventh grade, Peter."

His brother laughed and rolled his eyes. "Yeah, never could have done it without you, bro."

"So Isabel will have a cousin to play with," Elise said. "How many months apart in age will they be?"

"Well, Isabel was one year old in early August so…" Michelle paused to count off fingers.

Elise blinked and flashed an intrigued smile at Jared. "Really? What day? Grace was born on August tenth."

August tenth? That was Isabel's…

Jared's chest seized. The apprehension that had haunted him since Elise's phone call that morning reared its head, nipping the nape of Jared's neck with a tingle of alarm.

"That's—" Michelle started.

"The *sixth*," Jared said, cutting her off, his tone firm and unyielding.

"What?" Peter wrinkled his nose. "Jeez, man. Can't you even remember your daughter's birthday? It's the tenth, too."

Restless anxiety stirred in his gut. "No. That's…that's just when we had her party this year. Her, uh…birthday is the sixth, and we picked her up on the eighth. I'm sure of it."

Michelle and Peter exchanged glances.

"That's not how I remember—"

Jared forced a laugh, interrupting Michelle again. "Do you want me to get out her birth certificate to prove it?"

Peter scowled at him. "What's your problem?"

Elise raised both hands. "Whoa. I didn't mean to start a family squabble." She sent Jared a puzzled side glance, then beamed at her hosts. "Congratulations. I'm thrilled for you. I hope to have good news of my own to announce before long."

Michelle raised her eyebrows. "Oh? That sounds intriguing. Any hints?" She shot Jared a speculative glance. "Jared?"

Masking the frenzy of unease roiling inside him, Jared twitched a cheek. "Don't look at me."

Peter leaned close to his niece and asked in a stage whisper, "Izzy, do you know Elise's big secret?"

"Ba!" Isabel held up her pea-caked hand, showing it to her uncle.

He pulled back to avoid getting smeared with green. "No thanks, honey. I have my own."

"Let's just say I'm hopeful that a project I recently undertook may come to fruition soon." Elise reached over to wipe Isabel's hand, and the motherly gesture sent Jared's thoughts spiraling.

Isabel and Elise had a lot of physical similarities. Isabel and Grace were born on the same day. Grace was sent to Second Chance for black-market adoption.

Panic swelled in Jared's chest, pressing on his lungs until he couldn't breathe. He wished he could write those truths off as coincidence, ignore the facts that were screaming for his attention.

But Jared didn't believe in coincidence.

And he had precious little time to decide what he was going to do before Elise caught the scent of his suspicions.

Chapter 11

Throughout dinner and on the ride home from his brother's house, Jared seemed distracted, distant. Elise told herself it was just nerves over having his family meet her. Where a couple weeks ago she'd agreed to pretend to be his girlfriend, it was clear to both of them that something real and meaningful was blossoming between them. The changes in their relationship had her asking hard questions about what she wanted, where she saw their future, so she couldn't blame him for his reticence.

After he sighed and shifted restlessly in the driver's seat for the fifth time in ten minutes, she reached over and covered his hand on the steering wheel, giving him a comforting squeeze. "Want to talk about it?"

He jerked his gaze to hers. "About what?"

She lifted a shoulder. "Whatever has you so antsy tonight." She tipped her head in query. "Is it me?"

Perhaps it was a trick of shadows in the dim car, but Elise could have sworn he flinched at the suggestion.

"Why would you say that?" His voice didn't sound right to her. Was it nerves? She knew men hated talking about feelings, about relationships. Maybe pressing him for answers was putting him on the spot. She didn't want him to think she was looking for promises or commitments he wasn't ready to make. She wasn't sure she was at that stage yet, either.

Sure, she cared for him. Deeply. And she'd grown attached to Isabel, as well. But if events played out as she hoped, as MysteryMom indicated they might, Elise was about to have a baby in her life, a daughter with whom she needed quality time to bond and care for. Now might not be the best time to start a romantic relationship with Jared.

Perhaps Jared had even realized that himself and was uncertain how to broach the topic with her. After all, he'd started acting odd just after she'd called him about MysteryMom's progress in tracking Grace to the adoption agency called Second Chance.

"Well, tonight was a pretty big step," she said. "You know, formally introducing the new girlfriend to the family. And not even the fake new girlfriend. I mean, it's pretty obvious there's something between us, something more than the last few nights of sex."

He slanted another meaningful glance toward her, his jaw tight.

"Don't get me wrong. The sex has been great."

That earned her a quick, lopsided grin of agreement, but still he made no comment.

"The last couple nights have been…special to me," she continued, filling the silence. "And I've been giving our future together a lot of thought—where we are going with this, the timing—so I understand if you're having mixed feelings or asking yourself a lot of questions, too."

He pulled the car into his driveway and cut the engine. With a glance in the rearview mirror, he checked on Isabel, who'd fallen asleep in her car seat on the drive home. He turned his body to face her, resting his arm on the steering wheel. "I'm sorry if I've been acting weird today. I… have a lot on my mind. Not just about you, although I have been thinking about us, too. Wondering if I'm really ready for another relationship."

"Oh." Elise withdrew her hand and sat back in the seat. She felt her protective walls slam into place. A voice in her head shouted that retreat was her best defense, and she quickly steeled herself for what was coming.

Clearly he sensed her withdrawal, and he cupped her face. "Hey, that's not my way of breaking up with you. I would never have made love to you if I didn't have feelings for you. I just don't know what to do with those feelings yet."

Her resolve slipped a bit, and the tenderness of his touch chased some of the chill from her heart.

"No matter what happens in the next few days, I want you to know what you mean to me. You're a beautiful, strong, caring woman, and you've made me believe real love can happen twice in a lifetime." He stroked her chin with his thumb, and his dark gaze burrowed to her soul. "If things were different, I know I could fall in love with you. And maybe in time I will. But—"

"Wow," she cut in, catching his hand between hers and clasping it between her palms. "For someone who says he's not breaking up with me, that sure sounded like a goodbye."

"Uh, no… I just—" He lowered his eyes and sighed heavily. "Forget it. Like I said, I'm tired, and I have a lot on my mind. Ignore me. I—" He glanced to the backseat. "Let's get Sleeping Beauty inside and settled in. Okay?"

Without waiting for a response, Jared climbed from the front seat and opened the back door to unbuckle Isabel from her car seat. Puzzling over his odd mood, Elise gathered her purse while he carefully lifted the dozing baby onto his shoulder.

"I'll get her diaper bag. You go on in," she offered.

Once in the house, Elise fed the hungry cats that greeted them at the door while Jared put his daughter to bed. She bent to stroke Brooke's back while her kitty chowed down her dinner. "Are you getting along with your new friends, Brookie Wookie?"

Brooke leaned into Elise's hand as she scratched the cat's neck, and Elise took that as an affirmative. No hissing between the cats at dinnertime was progress.

Leaving the felines to their food, she sat down in the living room to wait for Jared. When he didn't come back out for several minutes, she wandered down the hall in search of him. She found him standing beside Isabel's crib, stroking her head and watching her sleep.

Tiptoeing up beside him, she whispered, "Is everything all right?"

He drew a deep breath that sounded choked with emotion. "Yeah."

Elise smiled, touched by the sweet innocence of the slumbering child. "She's precious."

"She's my world, Elise. I would never have survived losing Kelly if I hadn't had Isabel. I poured all of my grief into taking care of Izzy and giving her all the love I had." He raised a penetrating look to Elise. "I need her. She's a part of me. I couldn't bear to live without her."

Elise frowned. His boldly direct comments frightened her. "Jared, what's going on?"

"I just wanted you to know that."

She nodded. "I think most parents feel that way. I know I felt it for Grace. I *still* feel that way about Grace."

With a furrow in his brow, he jerked a nod and pivoted away from the crib. Elise followed him back to the living room where he flopped on the sofa and leaned his head back on the cushions. "You don't need to wait up for me if you're ready for bed. I'm going to stay up for a while and do some work, catch up on some bills."

A cool draft raised goose bumps on her skin, and she folded her arms over her chest to ward off the chill that burrowed to her heart. She was being dismissed. Jared clearly wasn't ready to share whatever was bothering him with her. After the intimacies they shared the last couple nights and the open book she'd made of her life, especially in regard to her grief over and search for Grace, Jared's unwillingness to open up to her felt like a snub. And the snub stung.

Elise turned without a word and left him alone and brooding. She changed out of her work clothes and slipped on an oversized T-shirt of Jared's she'd been sleeping in the last few nights—when she'd worn anything at all.

She lay on her side staring at the glowing numbers of the alarm clock on Jared's night stand for hours, waiting for him to join her in his big bed. A vast lonely ache filled her, and she longed to feel his arms around her. Amazing how quickly you could grow accustomed to having some-one beside you, savoring his warmth and reassurance as you slept.

Eventually, despite her own restless thoughts about Jared, MysteryMom, Grace and Isabel, Elise drifted to sleep. The next thing she knew, her internal alarm woke her at 6:00 a.m., and she rolled over to find Jared's side of his bed empty. The pillow bore no dent indicating he'd ever slept there last night.

Pain slashed through her, along with worry over what was troubling Jared and a premonition of what it might mean to their future. She smoothed a hand over his pillow, burying her nose in the sheets to inhale his lingering sandalwood scent. The hollow ache that swelled in her chest forced her to admit her feelings for Jared were deeper than she'd wanted to believe.

She was in real trouble. Just as he was pulling away, she had figured out how much she cared for him. How much she'd come to rely on his support and companionship. She'd dared to trust in him.

She was falling in love with him.

Tossing back the covers, she swung her legs to the floor and made her way to the kitchen where the mellow aroma of fresh coffee brewing told her Jared was awake.

When she found him in the kitchen, he was staring out the window over the sink, a steaming mug clutched between his hands and a forlorn expression on his face. He still wore the same clothes from the night before, and the dark smudges under his eyes spoke of his lack of sleep.

Elise's concern for him spiked. "Jared?"

He jolted as if he hadn't heard her come in. She stepped up behind him, circling him with her arms and laying her cheek on his back. "Did you get any sleep at all?"

"I dozed a few minutes here and there." He covered her hand and gave her fingers a squeeze before pulling away. At the door to the living room, he paused. "I made coffee. Help yourself."

"Thanks." She poured herself a mug and strolled into the living room to join him.

Jared sat on the couch with a laundry basket at his feet and—Elise did a double take—a half-full suitcase lying open beside him. As he folded the laundry, he put the clothes, both his and Isabel's, in the suitcase.

A beat of apprehension made her pulse stumble. "Going somewhere?"

He looked up briefly, then returned his attention to his task. "Afraid so. Family emergency out of town. I don't know how long I'll be."

"Oh, no. I'm sorry to hear that." An odd combination of concern and relief tangled in her chest. Maybe Jared's odd behavior last night had to do with the family emergency and not her. Maybe his withdrawal was the way he dealt with stress, not an indication he was regretting the physical turn in their relationship. "What kind of emergency?"

He hesitated, a pair of Isabel's stretchy pants in his hand, but didn't look up. "A death. In Kelly's family."

"Oh, I'm sorry." She cradled her mug, a nervous uncertainty crawling through her. She wanted to do something to help or comfort him, but he still seemed so remote.

"You, uh…can stay here while I'm gone. It's safer for you here." He dumped a pile of socks on the couch and started sorting them.

Elise's stomach see-sawed. The prospect of being alone, whether in Jared's house or her own, unsettled her. Especially while the members of the black-market ring were being rounded up by MysteryMom's team. She'd lived alone for years, yet she'd never felt as vulnerable and isolated as she did now facing Jared's imminent departure. She was amazed how much she'd come to count on his reassuring presence, his strength and comfort, after just a few days with him.

She circled the sofa and sat beside him. "Why didn't you say anything last night?"

"I, uh…just got the call a couple hours ago."

She frowned. "I didn't hear the phone ring."

"I had my phone on vibrate." He shoved a few pairs of socks into the suitcase without looking at her.

"Oh." She sighed, the jittery sense that something wasn't right skittering through her veins. "Jared, are you sure—"

A cry filtered down the hall from Isabel's room. Jared jerked his head up, his body tensing. He started to rise from the couch, but she put a hand on his shoulder and pushed him back down. "Sit. I'll get her. It's the least I can do to help."

He cast her an uncertain look but finally nodded. "All right. Thanks."

Elise put her mug on the coffee table and headed down the hall to the nursery. Isabel stood in her crib whimpering groggily and rubbing her eyes. Elise smiled at the little girl's disheveled mop of blond curls and the faint impression of rumpled bedding still etched in her cheek. "Good morning, sunshine."

Isabel blinked at her, appearing a bit confused, then raised an arm to Elise, asking to be picked up.

Warmth tugged Elise's heart as she lifted Isabel into her arms and cuddled her close. But one sniff, one glance at Isabel's diaper confirmed that the baby needed a complete change before starting her day. Elise wrinkled her nose and made a silly face for Isabel. "Eew. Stinky-poo. Someone needs a clean diaper."

Isabel grabbed her nose and wrinkled her face, imitating Elise, then grinned broadly.

Elise chuckled and laid Isabel on the changing table. "You're a silly goose, Izzy."

After pulling off Isabel's pajama bottoms and diaper, Elise carefully cleaned and rediapered her, then took out a fresh set of clothes from the drawer beneath the changing table. "How about pink stripes today? This is a cute outfit."

Isabel squirmed, uninterested in the new clothes and clearly eager to be finished with the changing table.

"Okay, I'll hurry, wiggle bug." After removing the dirty pajama shirt, Elise fumbled one-handed with the new shirt while she steadied Isabel with the other hand. As she raised the pink top to pull over Isabel's head, she glimpsed something that made her heart stop.

Isabel had a birthmark on her right shoulder.

A red, pear-shaped birthmark.

Her mind stalled for a moment, too stunned to process what she was seeing. But as a shot of adrenaline sped through her blood, her brain worked overtime, piecing together a staggering truth. She stared at Isabel. The same age her daughter would be. Blond-haired. Adopted.

"Oh, God..." she rasped, shaking to her core.

Isabel was Grace.

A joy, sweet and pure, flooded her heart, and tears pricked her eyes as she drank in the sight of her daughter as if for the first time. "Grace...oh, Grace!"

She scooped her daughter into her arms and held her close, raining kisses on her mussed hair and laughing. "Oh, my God. Oh, Grace, it's you. I can't believe it!"

Spinning toward the door, she hurried down the hall to the living room, eager to share the wonderful news with Jared.

"Jared! Jared, she's Grace. Isabel is Grace! She has a birthmark on her shoulder just like Grace's." She laughed again, swiping happy tears from her eyes. "Isn't it crazy and wonderful? All along, Grace was Isabel! I—"

She stopped short, realizing Jared didn't look at all happy. He looked...stunned. No, worse. Terrified. Defensive even.

Frowning, she took a mental step back and tried to see the news through his eyes. Of course he was scared, confused, worried. He had to be wondering what this would mean for him and his family. It was a lot to process. A lot to—

Then, like a storm cloud rolling in to spoil a picnic, more realizations clicked into place, darkening her mood.

Jared's withdrawal after learning the name of the adoption agency.

The lies he'd told her about Isabel's mother, her birth date, her adoption.

She stared at Jared, taking in his combative stance, his guilty expression, the bleak desperation in his eyes.

Elise's stomach knotted, and fury flashed through her. "You knew."

His nostrils flared as he inhaled deeply and raised his chin. But he didn't deny it.

She clutched Grace closer to her chest. "You *knew,* and you lied to me to throw me off track!"

When he remained silent, she aimed a finger at him. "You used Second Chance to adopt Isabel, didn't you? Didn't you!"

Again his silence damned him, and her hurt and anger swelled. "You knew who Isabel really was as soon as I told you about Second Chance yesterday. That's why you were so distracted and upset last night."

His jaw tightened. "I suspected, but I—"

She gasped as her gaze darted to the suitcase and more truths snapped into focus. "There was no death in the family. Was there?"

He said nothing.

"You were going to run with her, go into hiding—"

"Elise, listen to me…" He took a step toward her, and she took a step back, protectively wrapping both arms around the child she now knew was her flesh and blood.

"You were going to kidnap her to keep me away from her, weren't you?" she asked, acid roiling in her gut.

"It wouldn't be kidnapping. She's my daughter. I have every right to—"

"You have *no* right!" Elise shouted, and Grace jerked, startled, then began crying. Elise stroked her daughter's head and swayed with her, trying to calm her baby. "Shh, sweetie. It's okay."

Keeping her voice pitched low, she grated, "You betrayed me. I trusted you with my deepest heartache, and you betrayed me!"

Jared shook his head. "No."

"What do you mean, no? You lied to me! You told me her birth mother was a teenager in Lake Charles!"

He spread his hands, his eyes fiery. "That was what Second Chance told us. I had no reason to doubt them."

"You lied last night about when she was born and again this morning about a family emergency…"

He gave a humorless laugh. "I'd call this an emergency."

She gaped at him, so hurt and angry and staggered by the turn of fate, that she didn't know where to begin making sense of it all. For his part, Jared only stared back at her, a myriad of emotions playing over his face.

"You know you can't leave town with her," she said finally.

"I know no such thing." His tone was flat and unyielding.

"Jared?" A fresh fear pushed in from the edges of her anger. She could still lose Grace. If Jared left the state with her…fled the country.

Protective instincts roared through her. New tears filled her eyes, and she hated the position Jared was forcing her to take. "I'll call the police if you so much as leave this house with her."

His hands fisted, and he took another step toward her. "We legally adopted Isabel."

"How can you say that when I never gave her away? She was stolen from me!"

"We signed papers and filed documents with the court. In the eyes of the law, Isabel is *my* daughter."

"You would try to keep her from me?" Elise asked, galled and sickened by the notion.

His jaw tightened, and he growled through clenched teeth, "I'll do whatever I damn well have to in order to keep my daughter—"

"She's my daughter!" Elise shouted, losing the battle to keep the writhing whirlwind of emotions bottled up.

Grace wiggled hard, still crying, and Elise loosened her hold, allowing her daughter to pull away from her embrace. Grace twisted at the waist, spotted Jared and lunged for him, arms extended. "Da-dee!"

He took a giant step forward to catch Grace, and Elise had no choice but to release her grasp on her daughter if she didn't want to start a tug-of-war over the baby. Seeing her daughter tuck her head against Jared's chest, whimpering and clinging to his shirt, wrenched Elise's heart.

Jared was the father Grace knew, loved and trusted. Would moving her to a new home with a new parent do irreversible harm to Grace? In time, Grace would love and trust her, too, Elise knew, but would there be a hole in her daughter's heart where Jared should have been?

I need her. She's a part of me. I couldn't bear to live without her.

Jared's comments from last night made sense to her now. He was pleading with her, laying the groundwork for what would be an emotional uphill battle between them over a baby they both loved.

Elise wrapped her arms around her middle, feeling as if

she had to physically hold herself together or she'd crumble any minute. How could she be so close to having Grace back and yet still have her biggest hurdles in front of her?

The open suitcase on the couch caught her eye, reminding her that Jared had been willing to play dirty, to leave town with Grace rather than surrender her. He'd lied to keep Elise from learning the truth. He'd realized who Isabel was and said nothing, despite knowing the depths of grief Elise had been through over losing her daughter and her desperation to get Grace back.

Gritting her teeth, she shoved down the tug of sympathy for Jared's dilemma and firmed her resolve. She met the hard and determined stare he sent her over the top of Grace's head. His stony expression told her he had already dug his heels in and was prepared to go the distance.

"I think you should leave now," he said in a monotone that brooked no resistance.

An icy disappointment and anguish pierced her soul, but she lifted her chin and blinked back her tears. If he wanted a fight, she'd give him one. "Not without my daughter."

"Isn't going to happen."

Acid pooled in Elise's stomach. This was *so* not how she wanted to handle their impasse. But as she looked into Jared's eyes, the compassion for her heartache that had drawn her to him in the past weeks was secondary to his steely resolve. The tenderness and affection for her that she'd experienced as they made love had been shoved aside for stubborn conviction, defensiveness…and fear. A fierce, gripping fear like that of a wounded, trapped animal who would fight his predators to the death. A fear she knew well, because it was rooted in parental love.

With a grieved sigh, she marched over to the kitchen chair where she'd left her purse. Slinging the purse strap over her shoulder, she returned to the living room and faced Jared with squared shoulders. "Leaving town with her will only hurt your case. You don't want criminal charges against you, so please don't force my hand on that issue."

He remained still and stoic, his hand gently patting Grace's back as she snuffled against his shoulder.

Elise stepped forward to stroke and kiss her daughter's head. "I love you, Grace."

Turning on her heel, she walked to the front door and paused with her hand on the knob. "You'll be hearing from my lawyer."

Chapter 12

The click of his front door closing behind Elise echoed hollowly through Jared's house…and his heart. He hadn't felt this empty and bereft since the highway patrol officer and chaplain left him sitting on his sofa, staring blankly into space on the night of Kelly's accident.

That day, he'd lost his wife. Today, he stood to lose even more. Not only could the courts side with Elise and take Isabel from him, but he feared he'd already lost a bright and vibrant woman with whom he'd fallen in love.

Elise's anger with him for the lies and deception he'd stooped to were understandable. He wasn't proud of his actions, but he'd felt cornered. His desperation to protect Isabel had skewed his judgment.

But even lies were forgivable, given time. Yet the hurt and betrayal he'd seen in her eyes bore witness to the deep wound he'd inflicted with his choices. He knew Elise's history, the value she placed on trust. He'd let her down, and he regretted to his marrow the pain he'd caused her. Regretted even more that in order to keep Isabel, he'd have to inflict more pain on Elise.

He hated the antagonistic and divisive tone of his confrontation with Elise. This wasn't the way he'd wanted to handle their stalemate. Hostility between them benefited no one. Least of all Isabel. Yet battle lines had been drawn, and he was afraid the damage to his rapport with Elise had been done.

He heaved a weary sigh, full of guilt and frustration for the way he'd hurt Elise and put her on the defensive.

Isabel raised her head from his chest and blinked at him with her bright blue eyes. Elise's eyes.

And Elise's golden hair. Elise's pert nose. Elise's perfect bowed lips.

His lungs felt leaden. For the rest of his life, he would look at Isabel and see Elise. The woman who'd wakened his heart from the slumber of grief and shown him the possibility of second chances.

Second Chance. Futile anger streaked through him when the adoption agency popped into his mind. He and Kelly had trusted Second Chance much the way Elise had trusted Dr. Arrimand. There was no shortage of betrayal in this scenario.

The butterfly touch of damp baby fingers on his face roused him from his dark deliberations.

"Da-dee?"

He gave Isabel a sad smile. "Hey, princess."

She turned toward the kitchen and wiggled a chubby hand. "Eat nana."

His daughter was nothing if not a creature of habit. She had no use for her father's crises. Routine dictated she eat breakfast as soon as she woke up. Banana and dry Cheerios with a sippy cup of milk. His smile brightened, but a bittersweet ache lanced his chest as he smoothed her rumpled curls back from her eyes. "Sure, let's go eat banana."

Jared headed into the kitchen, praying this wouldn't be the last chance he had to eat breakfast with Isabel.

And knowing his first task after they ate was to call his attorney.

Elise sent a desultory glance about her ransacked apartment as she entered, dropping her purse on the coffee table. She'd been in no mood to clean house four days ago after being run off the road, visiting the E.R. and finding a burglar in her home, so she hadn't touched the mess. Now, her fight with Jared and last night's lack of sleep left her drained and despondent.

She slumped onto her couch and kicked off her shoes. Pulling a throw from the back of the sofa and wrapping it around her shoulders, she gave in to the tears she'd held at bay while driving home. She released the knot of frustration and hurt, anger and dejection that crowded her chest and clogged her throat. She berated herself for having allowed Jared to slip past her defenses and into her heart. Years of experience had taught her to be more circumspect and more discerning with her love and faith, yet she'd repeated the same mistakes again.

She was alone once more, nursing a bruised ego and a battered soul without even Brooke to give her comfort and companionship. She'd been so devastated by Jared's deception and so stunned by the discovery of Isabel's birthmark that she'd even stormed out without her cat.

She had no doubt she'd be able to safely retrieve Brooke soon enough. Her real concern was how long it would take the wheels of justice to clear the way for Grace to be returned to her. If Jared fought her for custody—correction, *when* Jared fought her for custody, because he'd made clear he would move heaven and earth to keep his daughter—he could drag the legal battle on for years.

Her doorbell pealed, and she stiffened. Her heartbeat accelerated as she moved her feet to the floor. Who in the world would visit her at this hour of the morning? Had Jared had a change of heart? Unlikely.

She thought of the thugs who'd run her off the road and broken into her house, but she dismissed the idea. Why would a criminal, intending to harm her, bother ringing her doorbell? Still, she looked for something to use as a weapon as she made her way to the foyer. Hoisting a heavy vase with one hand, she cracked the door open, keeping the security chain in place.

Her brother stood on the front porch, a box of doughnuts in his hand.

"Michael?"

He peered through the crack at her and gave her chagrined smile. "Yeah, I know. Surprised to see me."

"Hang on a second." She closed the door long enough to remove the security chain, then let him in.

Michael's gaze landed on the vase in her grip, and he arched an eyebrow. "You weren't thinking of using that on me, were you?"

She set the vase aside and sighed. "No, I... Why are you here?"

"I've been a little worried about you after that call a couple weeks ago, so I—" He stopped when he saw the upheaval of her living room, and he frowned. "Damn, Elise, what happened here?"

"Someone broke in and ransacked the place, looking for records I had."

His scowl deepened. "What kind of records?"

"Ones that prove Grace was never at the Pine Mill Hospital morgue." Elise placed her hand on her brother's arm, curling her fingers into the sleeve of his jacket. "Michael, I was right. She's alive. And I've *found* her."

He shook his head as if to clear it. "Excuse me?"

"Long story. And right now I've got to find a good family-law attorney and clean this place up and…" She raked her hair back from her face with her fingers, then looked up at her brother again. "Wait, you came by because you were worried about me?"

He arched an eyebrow. "You sound surprised. I'm your brother. Why is it strange that I'd worry about you?"

Fresh tears pricked her eyes. "Because I…you—"

"Haven't been a very good brother in the past?" he finished for her. He twisted his lips. "I know. And I can't promise I'll be much better in the future. You know I'm not good with emotional stuff, but…" He shrugged and shoved the doughnuts toward her. "I'm here now, and I brought breakfast. So…if you want to talk…"

She took the doughnut box and set it aside. "What I want is a hug. I've missed you."

She put her arms around his back, and he returned an awkward squeeze. "Okay, tell me what's been going on."

Grateful for the sounding board to help her sort out the past several days, Elise led Michael to the couch and told him the whole incredible story, starting with meeting Jared at the grief-support group. She'd made it as far as describing how she and Jared had walked in on the burglar in her house when her phone chimed, indicating a new email.

She scurried from the couch to retrieve the phone from her purse, then returned to sit by her brother. Her pulse spiked when she saw who'd sent the email. "It's from MysteryMom."

Michael scooted closer to read the email over her shoulder. "You mean you still don't know who this woman is?"

She waved him off. "She has to protect her identity

because of the work she does. I trust her." Her chest
clenched as soon as she spoke the words.

You trusted Jared, too, and look where that got you.

"So what does she say?" Michael wiggled his hand,
hurrying her.

Steeling herself with a deep breath, Elise thumbed the
key to open the email.

Progress! The federal agents working with me raided
Second Chance and seized their records. I've narrowed down the list of possible adoptive parents to
three names.

Elise didn't have to read the list to know Jared and Kelly
would be one of the couples. But seeing the confirmation
of her suspicions glowing on her phone sent a shiver to
her core. MysteryMom had the paperwork to support her
case to reclaim Grace.

With a heavy heart, she typed, Jared and Kelly Coleman adopted Grace. I know because Jared is the man
I've been dating.

The man I love. The man who betrayed me.

As briefly as she could, Elise laid out the facts of how
she met Jared, how she'd just found Isabel's birthmark and
how he planned to oppose her in court. With a sad sigh,
she hit the send key.

Michael repositioned himself to face her on the sofa.
"So this guy you were seeing knew he had your daughter, and he slept with you without saying anything about
what he knew? What a jerk!" He pulled a sympathetic grin.
"Want me to beat him up for you?"

Elise frowned. "No. And I don't recall saying we slept
together."

He tipped his head. "Really? You didn't?"

She rolled her eyes. "We did. But I don't think he realized what was going on until afterward. He said it was when I told him about Second Chance that he put it together."

"Jeez, Elise, what have you gotten yourself involved in?" Michael rocked back against the sofa cushions and buzzed his lips as he exhaled. "Federal agents? Black-market rings? Sounds like I was right to worry about you."

She hummed an acknowledgment, then tossed her phone on the coffee table and flopped back on the sofa pillows. A weight sat on her lungs, and thoughts of Jared made her throat thicken with tears. "What a mess."

"Yeah. Look, I know you didn't ask for my advice, but if I were you, I'd insist on DNA tests. You're gonna need every shred of proof you can get when you go to court."

Elise bit down on her bottom lip, knowing her brother was right. "I hate to think of them poking poor Grace for her blood."

Michael shook his head. "No blood. They can use a cheek swab nowadays. Completely painless."

She lifted an eyebrow. "And you know this because…?"

He chuckled. "Hey, not what you're thinking! I gave a DNA sample when I registered for the bone-marrow donors registry."

"You did?" She managed a warm smile. "That's great." Tipping her head, she asked, "I don't suppose you also know a good custody attorney?"

"I don't. But I have a friend who might."

"Let's give him a call." She sat forward, reaching for her phone when it chimed that a new email had arrived. She pulled the email up and opened it.

"MysteryMom?" Michael asked.

She nodded as she read aloud for Michael's benefit. "Unfortunately, your visit to Pine Mill Hospital and the raid last night at Second Chance have sent the rest of the people involved in the black-market ring scattering like roaches when the light is turned on. We have arrest warrants for all the scum involved, but we haven't rounded everyone up yet."

Michael grunted and scrubbed a hand over his face. "That doesn't sound good."

"No, it doesn't." The last two lines of the email caught Elise's attention, and her neck prickled.

Be careful and continue to lie low. You're still in very real danger.

"You really don't have to stay with me. I'll be fine," Elise insisted, though her brother's offer touched her deeply.

Michael pulled on his jacket and opened the front door. "No arguments. We don't know what these people are capable of, and I'm not taking any chances." He gave her a level look. "I'll be back as soon as I can pack up a few things for overnight. Lock the door behind me."

"Yes, Mother," she quipped, and he made a face that said "smart-aleck."

After her brother left, Elise straightened the living room a bit, mustering the nerve to phone the attorney Michael's friend had recommended. When she finally made the call, the attorney's secretary simply made an appointment for Elise to come in later that afternoon to go over the case details with the lawyer.

Elise sat on the couch, shaking with nervous energy for several minutes after she disconnected. Dread made her feel as if she had concrete in her veins. She wished she could find a way to convince Jared that as Grace's birth mother, Grace *belonged* with her. Having her mother was in Grace's best interests.

She knew at some point the issue of joint custody would come up, but she balked at the idea. Some selfish part of her rebelled against giving up even a little time with her daughter. She'd already missed fourteen months of Grace's life. And after he'd planned to run away with Grace today, how could she trust Jared not to violate a custody arrangement and take off with her in the future?

She imagined what it would be like to have Grace here at her house, using the nursery she'd set up over a year ago. Would she ever be able to look at Grace and not think of her as Isabel? Not think of Jared?

Her cell phone trilled, and the caller ID flashed Jared's name. Her heart rose to her throat as she lifted the phone to her ear. "Hello."

"It's me. I…think we should talk."

Just hearing his voice made her ache with longing and regret. "I know."

"Things got out of hand this morning, and…before you call a lawyer—"

"I just did. I have a meeting later today."

His sigh hissed through the line. "Elise, don't do this."

An edge of defensiveness crept back into his tone, and her temper rose to meet it. "Don't do what? Fight for my daughter?"

"Look, we don't even have proof she is your daughter. You can't—"

"Actually I do have proof." She explained to him everything MysteryMom had said in her last email about the raid at Second Chance and how he and Kelly were one of three possible adoptive couples to have gotten Grace.

Her revelation met only silence from Jared.

Elise drew a deep breath. "And just to be absolutely sure, I want her DNA tested."

"What!"

"My brother assures me they can do it with a simple cheek swab now. It's quick and painless, and we can know for sure whether or not she's Grace."

"Elise, be reasonable. If we sit down and talk this out—"

"I am being reasonable, Jared. What's not reasonable about a mother wanting her child returned to her!" When he didn't answer, she checked to make sure the call hadn't been dropped. "Jared?"

"I'm here." The hopelessness that permeated his tone speared her heart.

"If you think we can talk without arguing again..." she finger-combed the hair off her forehead "...I'll come by after my meeting with the lawyer. I have to pick up Brooke anyway."

"I'll be here. I've taken a personal day to handle this."

"Okay." Her pulse fluttered foolishly at the notion of seeing Jared again. Didn't her heart realize he was the same man trying to take Grace from her permanently? She squeezed her eyes shut waiting for him to say goodbye, to hang up on her...*something.* Instead a heavy silence hung between them, vibrating over the cell connection and saying more than words could.

I hate this. I miss you. I'm sorry. But she said none of it. As much as it hurt to be at odds with Jared, Grace was her priority, and she couldn't let her ill-conceived feelings for Jared stand in the way.

Finally, he heaved a sigh. "Where's Solomon when you need him, huh?"

Elise frowned. "Solomon?"

"You know, the king in the Old Testament. When two

women were fighting over a baby, he ordered the child cut in half."

She nodded even though she knew he couldn't see. "Oh, right. Him." She dragged herself off the sofa and crossed the floor to stare out a window where a gentle rain had begun to fall. "I should go. I still have to call my boss and explain why I'm not coming in today."

After hanging up with Jared, his comment echoed through her head.

Solomon. Two women.

In the Bible, the real mother had given up her claim on the baby to save her child's life, had sacrificed her right to the infant out of deep abiding love. And Solomon had known, by her sacrifice, who the real mother was.

Jared paced across his living room, jangling the change in his pocket, anxiety and doubt knotting his gut.

"What's going on?" Peter perched on the edge of the couch and shot him a troubled look. "You really scared Michelle on the phone. Is Isabel all right? Is she sick?"

He shook his head and fumbled for the right place to start. "It's about Elise."

"The lady you've been dating? Yeah, I like her. She's smart, pretty—"

"She's Isabel's mother."

Peter frowned and gave his head a little shake of confusion. "What? I thought you said Isabel's mother was a teenager in Lake Charles."

"That's what we were told. We were lied to. Scammed."

"And you know this how?"

"I've been helping Elise find out what happened to her baby ever since she got an email from this woman who calls herself MysteryMom, claiming that Elise's baby didn't die after birth like she'd been told."

Peter eased back on the sofa, his expression dark and wary. "Hell. I see where this is going."

Jared explained everything that had happened in the past few weeks, from Elise being run off the road and her home searched to the latest revelations about Second Chance.

"Not all of the children come through the black market, but MysteryMom found proof that Second Chance had an arrangement with Arrimand. When they find a desperate and gullible couple like us—" He didn't bother hiding his disgust and irritation "—They had an elaborate system in place for securing all the falsified documents to cover their tracks."

"And you've seen proof that Elise's baby was stolen? That Isabel was a black-market baby? Specifically *her* baby?"

Jared sighed and stopped in front of the window to stare at a bird chirping on an oak tree in the yard. His throat tightened with guilt over all he'd hidden from Elise. "I've had suspicions for days. Too many things matched up to be coincidence." He blew out a deep breath and raked both hands through his hair in frustration. "But I didn't say anything to Elise, because I wasn't sure, and... I didn't want to believe it was true."

He faced his brother, the same heartsick dread filling him that had guided his actions the past few days. "Then, this morning, Elise heard from MysteryMom that her agents working the case had narrowed down the number of families that could have gotten Grace to three. We were one of the couples on her list."

"But that's not—"

"This morning Elise was changing Isabel's clothes. She took Izzy's shirt off and saw the birthmark on Isabel's shoulder. She swears Grace, her daughter, had a birthmark just like Isabel's."

Peter shook his head and held up his hands. "Lots of babies have birthmarks. That's not—"

"She saw the birthmark *before* she heard from MysteryMom. She didn't know about Isabel's birthmark until today, but now Elise is convinced." Jared resumed pacing. "She's planning to see a lawyer to get Grace back even as we speak."

Peter cursed and scrubbed a hand over his face.

"And if the birthmark and the evidence MysteryMom found aren't enough to win her case, Elise wants a DNA test to prove she's Isabel's biological mother."

"Can she force you to comply?" his brother asked.

Jared stopped his restless wandering and slumped down in a recliner. "She doesn't have to. All you have to do is look at the two of them together and it's obvious. Isabel looks like Elise. She responds to Elise as if she instinctively knows there's a physical bond between them." A razor-like sorrow flayed his heart, and defeat settled on him, dark and heavy. "How do I let Isabel go? I don't think I can stand losing her on top of Kelly."

And Elise. The knife of despair already buried in his chest twisted, digging deeper.

He'd fallen in love with Elise, and now, because he'd tried to avoid the truth, tried to protect Isabel, he'd lost Elise's trust and respect. She'd filed him in the same category as the other monsters who'd conspired to steal her daughter. Not that he blamed her. If someone had tried to keep him from finding Isabel, he'd be livid, as well.

"You can't seriously be considering giving Isabel up. Hire your own lawyer! Fight her! You're Isabel's father, dammit!"

He faced Peter. "Maybe in my heart, but not biologically. She has the advantage."

"But your adoption—"

"Was arranged through fraud and kidnapping and—"

"You had no knowledge of any of those crimes." Peter aimed a finger at him to punctuate his point. "You adopted her in good faith."

Jared scoffed. "Do you really think a judge is going to give a flip about my intentions or my good faith?"

Peter shoved to his feet. "But it's been more than a year."

"Elise never gave permission for the adoption! Her baby was *stolen* from her. She was lied to. She believed Grace was dead." The agonizing truth landed in his chest like a wrecking ball. "She has every right to claim her daughter."

Now Peter paced the floor. "There's gotta be something you can do!" He pivoted on his heel and aimed a finger at Jared. "Run. Take Isabel and disappear. Go to another state."

He gave his brother a weary glance. "I considered it. Was prepared to do just that this morning right before Elise figured out the truth." Guilt gnawed his gut. "But kidnapping Isabel and becoming a fugitive isn't the answer."

Peter turned up a hand in concession. "I suppose you're right." He paced away then spun back toward Jared, his face brightening. "Oh, my God. It's so obvious! You care about Elise, right? I mean, the night you were over here it was pretty clear you'd fallen for her."

A bittersweet pang plucked his heart. "I love her."

"Perfect! So marry her and Isabel comes, too, as part of the package."

A fragile hope blossomed in Jared's soul, warming him from the inside out. Before she'd discovered his cover-up, Elise had seemed happy with him. Though she'd never voiced her feelings, he believed she'd cared for him, that she'd loved him. But he'd broken her trust, the very thing that had scarred her in past relationships and kept her from opening her heart to him unconditionally. He'd betrayed their friendship. Hoping that she'd forgive him and accept his proposal was a long shot.

Unless…

Maybe she'd give marriage a chance if he convinced her it was what was best for Grace.

Grabbing his keys from his pocket, he hurried to the front door. "Can y'all watch Isabel for a couple hours?"

Peter tailed him to the door. "Sure, but…where are you going?"

"To buy an engagement ring and find Elise."

Chapter 13

Elise couldn't sit still. Nervous energy pulsed through her veins, and her mind jumped from one thought to another, dragging her emotions on a roller coaster.

She needed to get Grace's nursery ready. Could she even change her name to Grace after she'd learned the name Isabel?

How long would it take to get a hearing scheduled? How could Jared have hidden the truth from her?

How could she take Isabel from the only parent she'd ever known? How could she take Jared's daughter from him?

How did she survive the ache of knowing someone else she loved had betrayed her? Had Jared known the truth about Isabel when he'd made love to her? He'd said he only suspected after hearing about Second Chance, but how could she trust anything he'd told her in light of his deception?

Would she be compelled to testify at Dr. Arrimand's trial? How long would it take to round up everyone involved? How long would she be in danger?

When would MysteryMom know—

Her doorbell pealed, interrupting her latest round of turbulent thoughts. Elise started for the door, assuming it was Michael returning as he'd promised.

"Elise? Are you there?"

Jared. Her mouth dried, and bittersweet anguish twisted her heart. She wasn't prepared to face him. Her emotions were too raw and unsettled.

"Please, Elise," he called through the closed door. "I know you're home. Let me in. We have to talk."

She yanked open the door. "Why are you here? I told you I'd come by your place after I talked to my lawyer."

"I know, but I have an idea to propose. I think we can figure this out so that we both win." His face was bright with optimism, and her spirits stirred with hopeful anticipation.

The prospect of a mutually agreeable solution intrigued her even though his choice of words bothered her. "We both *win?* Jared, this isn't a competition. Grace is not some prize to be won or lost!"

He held up a hand in concession. "Agreed. Poor choice of words. I'm sorry."

Elise studied him, and another piece of her anger toward him melted. He looked a mess. His hair was thoroughly ruffled, evidence he'd plowed his fingers through it numerous times today in frustration. Despite the light of optimism in his eyes, his face was lined and haggard. She remembered seeing a similar face staring back at her from her mirror in the weeks following the news that Grace had died. Now, he faced losing his daughter, and he was in hell.

A prick of empathy for his agony compelled her to let

him inside, despite the hurt and anger she harbored for his lies and silence. After shutting the door, Elise folded her arms over her chest as she faced him, holding herself together with her last threads of control. What she wanted was to throw herself into his arms and soak up the strength and security she'd relished in his embrace as recently as yesterday.

Meeting his dark gaze, she felt her heart crack just a little more. "Go ahead," she said, hoping he didn't hear the quiver in her voice.

"First of all, I'm sorry I didn't tell you my suspicions sooner. When I realized Isabel could be yours, I…was selfish. I could only think of what it would mean to lose her. I panicked."

"You said you have an idea to solve this?" she prompted without acknowledging his apology. She wasn't ready to forgive him yet. Too much was at stake. Her pain went too deep, and the cut was too new.

He flashed her an uneasy grin. "The answer is obvious, really. I'm her father. You're her mother."

She stared at him blankly, even though her brain was already miles ahead of him.

"If we lived together, Isabel could have both of us. We could share custody."

"Share her?"

"It makes sense, doesn't it?"

"Isn't that a bit like cutting her in half? Am I supposed to cry foul now and give her up rather than start a tug-of-war over her?"

"No tug-of-war, Elise. I'm suggesting we marry."

A patter of wistful yearning fluttered in her chest, but she kept her face impassive. No matter how much she longed for the kind of domestic bliss and family he described, she refused to settle for a marriage of convenience.

Grace deserved to be raised in a home where her parents loved each other as much as they loved her.

And I deserve to be loved for who I am, not just a means to an end.

"We don't have to turn this into a bitter and expensive custody battle with lawyers and judges, Elise."

She stiffened. "Is that what this is about for you? Avoiding the costs and hardship of a lawsuit?"

He shifted his weight, his expression uneasy. "I'd be lying if I said it wasn't part of my reasoning."

"Oh, but you're so good at lying." Her tone dripped sarcasm. "Why stop now?" The words slipped out before she could stop them, some cruel part of her wanting to hurt him the way he'd hurt her.

Jared flinched, and his face reflected the pain she'd inflicted.

Elise was shaking so hard she could barely stand. Dragging in a ragged breath, she slid to the floor. Tears blurred her vision, and bile filled her throat. What was she doing? This horrible situation wasn't Jared's fault. What kind of man, what kind of father would he be if he didn't fight for his daughter? She clutched her stomach, swallowing hard to force down the sour taste of anguish.

Jared stalked several steps away before shoving both hands through his hair and growling his frustration. "I'm sorry, Elise. I should have never lied to you. I should have leveled with you from the beginning, just like we promised each other. Brutal honesty. No pulling punches."

Then with a harsh exhale, he dropped his hands to his sides and crossed the floor to her. He crouched in front of her, his face shadowed with sadness. He reached for her before apparently thinking better of it and withdrawing his hand. "I didn't come here to fight with you. I don't want us to be adversaries in this."

"Neither do I."

His cheek twitched in a rueful grin. "That's good. Can we start over? Pretend this morning never happened?"

She sighed and averted her gaze, unable to bear seeing the turbulent emotion in his eyes any longer. "Jared…"

"I came here for a reason. I'm trying to fix this mess." He fumbled in his jacket pocket, and said, "I brought you this."

She angled a cautious glance to see what he had.

He held out a ring box, and the weight in her chest sank harder against her lungs. Under other circumstances, she'd be weeping tears of joy, cherishing this moment as a dream come true. But the moisture that leaked from her eyes was born of regret, her mind rebelling at the sight of the velvet box.

"Marry me, Elise. Marry me and raise Isabel with me." He cracked it open to reveal the diamond solitaire inside. A lovely ring, but not the one she'd dreamed of when she imagined this moment as a girl. Everything about his proposal felt wrong. His ring, his motive, his reasoning.

A sinking realization settled over her, clarifying what her instincts were saying. The ring he was offering had nothing to do with love. Not for her, anyway.

The courts would give Grace back to her, she was almost certain. In time, she'd have her daughter again, even if he put up a fight. His marriage proposal was rooted in his desperation to keep the baby he thought of as his daughter. He didn't want a wife. He wanted Isabel.

Tears puddled in her eyes, blurring her vision as she stared at him, willing him to say he loved her. Praying he'd give her some reason to believe in his feelings for her.

But he didn't.

"No."

"Elise?" he said, a note of panic creeping into his tone.

"Getting married is the perfect solution. And having both of us around is what's best for Isabel."

She swiped angrily at the moisture on her cheek. "Her name is Grace."

He opened his mouth, made a noise as if to reply, then fell silent as he met her level gaze.

She flipped the lid of the ring box closed and pushed it back toward him. "And don't pretend you're proposing marriage for any reason other than because it's what's best for you."

Disappointment and frustration lined his face, and he shook his head in confusion.

"Elise, how can you say—?"

She shoved to her feet, pushing past him and scrubbing the tears from her cheeks with a sleeve. "Committing yourself to a relationship because it will spare you a custody fight may be enough reason for you to get married, but I can't do it. I need more from a marriage than convenience or simplified parenting."

"But Isa—*Grace*—" he lifted a hand in appeal as if his concession on her name would win him points "—needs both of us. I know I should have told you what I suspected sooner, but I was terrified of losing my daughter."

Elise shook her head, giving him a sorrowful look. "You're still scared. That's the only reason you're here. And that's why I have to say no."

"Elise, that's crazy. At least think about—"

She stiffened, insulted by his insinuation that she was acting irrationally. "I want you to go now. We have nothing left to discuss."

He didn't move, but his jaw tensed, and she could see him mentally scrambling for an argument that would change her mind. "Elise, don't—"

"No. Leave." She aimed a finger at her door. "Now."

He straightened to his full height, whether to intimidate her or not she wasn't sure.

"Elise, what else do you want me to say?"

Say you love me.

"I've apologized for not telling you—"

"Goodbye, Jared." She stalked to the door and yanked it open, hiding behind her anger so that she didn't crumble in front of him. "My lawyer will be in touch. Please don't make this any harder than it already is for either of us."

His hands fisted, and he tightened his mouth to a grim line. "Not a chance." He stormed to the door and stopped in the threshold to lean in close to her and growl, "If this is the way you want it, fine. I don't care how hard it gets. I will fight with everything I've got to keep Isabel."

Jared drove home with his hands clenching the steering wheel and his gut roiling with fear, disappointment and self-disgust. Why had he let Elise provoke him to say such argumentative things? He didn't want her as an adversary.

He wanted to marry her. He cared deeply for Elise. More than he thought he'd ever care for another woman after losing Kelly.

Elise's skepticism and anger were understandable considering the way he'd misled her and avoided telling her the truth as soon as he realized who Isabel was. Antagonizing her was not a good game plan.

Jared parked in his driveway and dropped his forehead to the steering wheel. Why had he issued that parting shot about fighting with all he had for Isabel? Defensiveness was hardly the best way to work out an amicable custody agreement. *Stupid, stupid!*

His fear of losing control of the situation, of losing time to change her mind—hell, his fear of losing *Isabel*—had colored his response to Elise.

You're still scared. That's the only reason you're here.
And that's why I have to say no.

Elise had seen the truth, had known where his heart
was. But why did she think his desperation to keep Isabel
was grounds to reject his marriage proposal?

That's the only reason you're here.

Not so. Marriage made sense for them. It was the obvious solution.

I need more from a marriage than convenience or sim-
plified parenting.

But…their marriage would be about more than shared
custody. They had a good relationship, a growing friendship and sexual chemistry to spare. At least, he thought
so. What had he done to make her think he wouldn't be a
good husband?

Gritting his teeth, he shouldered open the car door and
stalked inside. Isabel was playing on the living-room floor,
and Michelle was folding laundry on the couch.

"Where's Peter?" Jared dropped his keys on the sofa
table and peeled off his jacket.

"He's picking us up a pizza." Michelle's face lit with
anticipation. "Well? What did she say? Can we reserve the
church for a wedding?"

"No." He dropped heavily in an armchair and scrubbed
a hand over his jaw.

Michelle frowned. "No…meaning no church, or—"

"No, meaning she said no. She turned me down flat."
The disappointment that had gnawed at him in the car
swelled into a sense of loss and defeat that left a hollow
ache in his soul. He hadn't considered for a minute that
she would refuse him, but her rejection stung more than
his pride. If he didn't save his relationship with Elise, he
stood to lose so much more than just his daughter. He'd
lose the woman he'd come to love.

"How could she say no?" Michelle pressed, shock filling her expression and her tone. "It's such a simple and obvious solution. You love each other, and you both love Isabel…what's the problem?"

He shrugged. "Hell if I know. I knew she was mad at me about the way things played out, and I apologized but… she wouldn't hear of it." He leaned his head back and shut his eyes, weary to the bone and heartsick. "Maybe she doesn't love me. I thought we were on the same page, but we never talked about our relationship in those terms."

"But you did tell her how you felt when you proposed… right?" Michelle asked hesitantly.

Jared's pulse skipped a beat as he replayed the conversation in his head.

"Jared Coleman—" Michelle's tone was stern "—please say you told Elise you loved her when you asked her to marry you."

His breath lodged in his lungs. "I…guess…not. I—"

The doorbell rang, interrupting his train of thought. Michelle stood, and he waved her back to the sofa. "I'll get it."

He hurried to the door, praying it was Elise. Praying he still had a chance to convince her of his feelings for her.

His heart in his throat, he yanked open the door. But instead of Elise, a linebacker-size man he'd never seen before stood on his porch.

Jared tensed. "Can I help you?"

The man looked past him to the living-room floor where Isabel played. "Jared Coleman?"

Jared raised his chin. "Who wants to know?"

"You have something that's not yours."

Before Jared could reply, the man lifted his hand and touched Jared's chest with a small black device. *A Taser!*

Every muscle and nerve in his body screamed in pain. Convulsed.

Michelle shrieked in terror.

Jared's vision dimmed, and he slumped to the floor.

Chapter 14

Pain.

Jared fought the light that stirred him. The light meant pain. In the darkness, he'd known sweet oblivion. He dragged a sore arm over his eyes to block the intruding light.

But with the light came sounds. Muffled noises that made the hair on his neck stand up. Whimpers. Frightened tears.

Adrenaline shot through him, reviving him with a jolt. "Isabel!"

He sat up quickly. So quickly his head rebelled with a throb that made him think his skull would explode. When the spots quit dancing in his vision, he blinked Michelle into focus.

She sat on the sofa, tied and gagged, with tears streaming from her eyes. She tried to talk, and he recognized the muffled sob that had woken him. He scanned the room, fear grabbing him by the throat.

Isabel was gone.

Fumbling to his knees, he crawled to Michelle and eased the gag from her mouth. "Where's Isabel?" he rasped.

"He took her," she cried. "I tried to stop him, but he was too strong for me. He overpowered me and tied me up."

"Pizza delivery!" Peter called as he breezed into the house. "Isn't it a bit cold outside to leave the door op—" He stopped short and frowned at Michelle. "Honey, what the hell is—"

"Isabel's gone. She's been kidnapped." Jared clambered to his feet, though his legs still felt rubbery. "Call the police!"

Eyes wide with alarm, Peter tossed the pizza box on the coffee table and picked up the cordless phone. "Is Elise behind this?"

Jared shook his head, then grabbed his temples. "I wish I could say she was. At least then I'd know my daughter was safe."

"Then who—?"

The phone in Peter's hand rang, and he answered it. "No, this is his brother. Hold on." He held the phone out to Jared with a scowl. "It's Elise. She says it's an emergency."

Sitting on her bathroom floor beside the commode, Elise rocked forward, clutching her stomach. She fought another wave of nausea as she waited for Jared to come on the line. Dear God, she had to get herself under control if she was going to be of any use to Jared or herself...any use to Grace.

"Elise? Talk to me." Jared's voice sounded strained, hoarse. *Oh, God, it was true!*

"Jared." Her voice cracked as she sobbed. "I had a call. They said they had Grace. I heard a baby crying and...tell me it wasn't her. Tell me—"

"I can't. A man showed up here and used a stun gun to knock me out. He overpowered Michelle and took Grace."

With a strangled cry, she leaned over the toilet and dry heaved.

"Elise? Are you there? What did they say in your call?"

She swiped her mouth with the back of her hand. "They want money. A lot of it. To fund their escape."

"Money. Of course."

"He said w-we only have twelve hours. The feds are hot on their trail, and...and they've got a plan to l-leave the country. Tonight. But they need cash." Elise drew a shuddering breath. "Oh, God, Jared...he said if we called the cops o-or didn't get the money or interfered in their escape in any way—"

A sob choked Elise.

"Tell me," Jared said.

"We'd never see Grace again."

Elise tensed when the doorbell rang, and she gnawed her lip as Michael answered it.

"Are you Jared?" he asked, blocking her view of the person on her porch.

"Yeah. Who are *you?*"

The sound of Jared's voice had Elise on her feet and racing to the door. She pushed Michael aside and threw herself into Jared's arms, all bitterness between them shoved aside in light of her terror for Grace. She needed the strength and reassurance his embrace offered more than she needed her next breath. He clung to her with the same fierce intensity that she squeezed him, clearly as distraught as she was.

"Have you reached MysteryMom yet?" he rasped.

"No," she said, her voice muffled against his chest. She angled her head back to meet the stark expression in his eyes. "I replied to her email, but she hasn't answered. Michael and I have been watching the Parents Without Children message board. So far, she hasn't signed on."

"You would be Michael, I presume?" Jared said.

"Yeah, her brother." Michael's tone was cool, but he offered a hand in greeting.

Jared released Elise in order to shake hands with Michael, then stepped inside, one arm around her shoulders.

"So what's our next move?" Michael asked, closing the door behind them.

Jared guided Elise to the couch and drew her down beside him. They exchanged a look of mutual worry and impatience, and her stomach knotted. Knowing Jared was just as helpless to save Grace as she was left an icy apprehension in her soul.

"I hate to say it, but given the deadline, we'd better start gathering the money they asked for." Jared rubbed his hands on the legs of his jeans. "We don't have time to wait for MysteryMom."

Nausea swamped Elise. "Jared, they want a quarter of a million dollars. Even if I wanted to pay them off—and I would if it would bring Grace home safely—I don't have anywhere near that much. I spent most of my savings on the treatments to get pregnant and have Grace in the first place."

Jared sighed. "Yeah, the adoption fee we paid Second Chance stripped most of our savings, too."

"I have about ten thousand saved up that you can have, Elise." Michael sat down in a chair across from them. "It's not much but…"

Tears flooded her eyes. "Thank you. Every little bit helps."

The room fell silent, a pervasive sense of the terrifying conundrum they faced hovered over them like a looming storm cloud.

"Maybe it's time we call the police," Michael said.

"No!" Jared and Elise said in unison.

Elise's chest tightened, fear battling common sense. "He said no cops."

Michael scoffed. "They always say no cops."

"We can't risk having them hurt Grace in retribution." Her voice shook, and she lunged to her feet to pace, to burn off restless energy. "They have to think we're cooperating."

"Elise, think about it. The police have experts in handling cases like this. If we don't—"

"No." Jared drilled a determined stare at Michael. "Not with Grace's life on the line."

Grace. Despite the turmoil facing them, the disquiet in her soul, Elise noticed Jared's use of Elise's name for her daughter.

Michael spread his hands in a conciliatory gesture. "Look, I know you both are scared for Grace, but you need to bring the authorities in on this."

"Not yet." Jared's tone matched the unyielding set of his jaw.

A cold tremor shook Elise to her marrow. She knew her brother was right, but she couldn't break free from the grip of terror. She kept replaying the menacing warning in the kidnapper's voice, and she hugged herself as a fresh wave of agony washed through her. Legs shaking, she dropped on the edge of a chair and put her head between her knees. "Ohgodohgodohgod," she moaned, her grief and worry a living thing clawing inside her. "My baby. They can't hurt my baby!"

She felt a warm hand on her back and raised her head to find Jared crouched beside her. She reached for him, and he drew her against his chest again.

"Please, Jared…please, don't let them hurt Gracie. Oh, God…"

His arms squeezed her tighter, and he kissed her head. "We'll find her, honey. Whatever it takes. I promise."

She wanted to ask how he could make such a pledge when the situation was so far out of their control, but instead, she grabbed his reassurance with both hands and held tight to it, needing to believe he was right.

After indulging in a few tears, Elise scrabbled her composure back together and swiped her cheeks with her sleeve. "I'm sorry. I'm just so scared."

"I know. Me, too." Jared dug his cell phone from his pocket and waved a hand toward her computer. "Why don't you check to see if MysteryMom is online yet, and I'll call my broker and see how much money I can raise if I sell my portfolio and cash in my retirement funds."

Michael scowled and massaged the back of his neck, but he said nothing.

Elise moved numbly to the table where she'd set up her laptop and refreshed the web page for the message board. No MysteryMom.

She drummed her fingers impatiently and racked her brain for another way to reach her anonymous patron. They were down to ten hours and change before their deadline with the kidnappers. Every minute of inaction ate at Elise, sawing her frazzled nerves.

She moved her hands to the keyboard and typed a pleading message to MysteryMom.

MysteryMom, help! EMERGENCY!!

With a click of the mouse, she posted the appeal and sat back in her chair.

All she could do was wait.

"I don't care if it bankrupts me!" Jared shouted into his phone as he stalked her living room like a caged tiger. "I'd pay twice that amount if it will bring my daughter home safely. Hell, I'd give my *life* if it would save hers."

Elise's breath snagged in her lungs. She watched Jared pace with her heart in her throat and a tender ache swelling inside her.

"Just do it, Henry." Jared's tone was grim and final. "Transfer all of it to one account, so we can wire it to their account when I give the go-ahead." He closed his eyes and pinched the bridge of his nose. "I understand. Just get it ready."

He thumbed the keypad on his phone and slumped back down on the couch, his body language full of defeat. "If I liquidate all my accounts, I can cover most of the ransom." He raised a weary gaze to Elise. "But we still need fifteen thousand."

Elise could only stare, dumbfounded.

"You're emptying all of your accounts?" Michael asked, his tone as stunned as Elise felt.

Jared nodded mutely, his attention still locked on Elise. "It's just money." He drew a deep breath and released it, his eyes growing damp. "Of course, this means I won't have the money to hire a lawyer. I won't be able to fight your custody suit."

Elise absorbed his admission like a fist to her gut. The breath she'd been holding wheezed from her, leaving her lungs aching and starved.

"But I'd give you custody a hundred times over to save

her from these thugs," he said, emotion strangling his voice.

A sob hiccupped from her throat.

King Solomon. Cut the baby in half. The real mother's sacrifice.

The love behind Jared's gesture dug deep into Elise's soul. His was the love of a parent, a father. A *real* father in every way that mattered. The sacrifice of all his funds, and thereby his means to claim custody, could be the difference between getting Grace back or not. The difference between life and death for her daughter. *Their* daughter.

Hollow acceptance of his fate darkened Jared's penetrating gaze, burrowing deep into Elise's heart. She knew the heartache he was suffering, because she'd lived it herself when she'd thought Grace had died. She lived it now, fearing for Grace's safety with the kidnappers. Jared was in a living hell. In a pain too deep and personal for words.

And she knew she couldn't be responsible for inflicting that level of agony and suffering on someone she loved.

Her pulse quickened. She loved Jared.

Maybe she'd known that all along, but she was certain now. She loved him if for no other reason than the depth of character and the love for his daughter that his generosity showed. Something shifted inside her, bringing a certainty she couldn't ignore into sharp, if painful, focus. She couldn't take his daughter away from him. No matter how much she loved Grace—perhaps because of how much she loved Grace—she could no longer justify removing her from the only home she'd ever known, from a father who adored her.

Maybe, if they could redeem their relationship when this nightmare was over, she might convince him to give her visitation rights. But Grace—no, *Isabel*—belonged with Jared.

"Jared, I want you to—"

The chime of her laptop cut her off as an instant message screen popped up. She turned toward the screen and caught her breath.

Jared surged off the sofa, crossing the floor in three long strides. "Is it her? Is it MysteryMom?"

"Yes." Elise trembled as she read the short message. Michael read over her shoulder, as well.

Elise, what's happened? What's your emergency?

Grace has been kidnapped. They've demanded money in the next 10 hours for her return.

She was shaking so hard with adrenaline and the swirl of emotions that she had to backspace and retype words a half dozen times.

"Here, let me." Jared nudged her aside, taking half the chair, and with fingers flying across the keyboard, he explained how he'd been knocked out and Grace stolen. He laid out the terms they'd been given and the warnings the kidnappers had issued about contacting the police.

Jared typed, We have most of the money ready to transfer to their account, but you have to pull your team back. Give us a chance to recover Grace before it is too late.

MysteryMom made no response for several nerve-racking seconds, then…

It's already too late.

Elise's heart stopped. With a gasp, she grabbed Jared's arm and dug her fingers into his wrist. "No…"

Another message popped up, and together they leaned close to the screen to read.

There are agents carrying out arrest warrants in three states even now. I can't pull anyone back without jeopardizing the whole mission. This case is bigger than just Grace. The people involved have side operations that include drug smuggling and human trafficking from Mexico, money laundering, bribery and intimidation of officials. They're accused of murder, kidnapping and child pornography. This is huge!

Jared rocked back, expelling a shaky breath. "Good God."

Elise typed, Dr. Arrimand is involved in all of this?

Heavens no. He was a pawn. His greed got him sucked into something bigger than he imagined and too dangerous to quit once he started. Same with his nurse.

Elise struggled for oxygen. What hope did they have for Grace against such odds, such a mammoth crime ring?

Jared stared at the floor, as still as a statue. His expression was pale, bleak.

Elise glanced at the framed ultrasound picture, the blurry white shape that was Grace at nine weeks' gestation. For so long, Elise had gazed at that picture and grieved for a child she'd believed dead. But a miracle had brought her baby back into her life, and she was far from ready to give up hope of finding Grace now.

Maternal love and protectiveness jabbed her, firing her determination, shaking her from her self-pity.

Elise typed to MysteryMom, I will NOT give up hope of getting Grace back.

I would never ask you to.

Jared cast a side glance at what she was typing.

So tell me what I can do. I won't just sit here while the clock ticks on the deadline the kidnappers gave us. I'll do whatever I must to get my daughter back!

Hang on. Let me consult with some of my team, and we'll come up with a plan. I'll message you within twenty minutes.

Eighteen excruciating minutes later, Elise hovered over her laptop, willing MysteryMom to return with a miracle solution. Across the room, Jared paced, his muscles tense and his mouth clamped in a grim line.

Little had been said since MysteryMom signed off to consult her colleagues, and Michael had disappeared into the kitchen to brew a pot of coffee no one wanted. Elise counted every tick of the clock, knowing each minute they waited was one less minute they had to find Grace before their deadline. Though she tried not to dwell on worst-case scenarios, her mother mind-set meant she couldn't help but fret over what would happen to Grace if the deadline passed. Would they kill her baby? Take her out of the country to be sold again? Use her in child porn and prostitution?

Her stomach rebelled at the thought, and bile rose in her throat. She squeezed her eyes shut, swallowing hard to force down the bitter taste and saying a silent prayer. *Please, oh, please, God, let Grace be all right!*

The chime of her laptop shattered the silence, and Elise

spun around on her chair to read the incoming message. Jared dashed over to sit beside her in a chair he'd pulled in from the kitchen. Their shoulders touched as they leaned in together to see the screen. Jared's familiar sandalwood scent filled her nose and managed to calm her to a degree. Knowing she wasn't facing this crisis alone mattered to her more than she could say.

What would it be like to always have someone beside her to face life's challenges and heartaches? To share her joys and the simple pleasures?

If they didn't rescue Grace in time, would she ever feel joy or savor any pleasures in life again?

Elise, are you there?

Jared and I are both here. What did you come up with?

We have an idea, but there are no guarantees it will work. It could prove costly to you.

Costly how?

We think, given our time constraints, that our best chance to track the men with Grace is to follow the money. Namely the ransom they've demanded. You said you could get most of it, right?

Elise glanced at Jared for confirmation, and he gave a quick, certain nod.

Between us, we can have all two hundred and fifty thousand dollars in a few hours.

Good. Before you authorize the money to be wired, we need the account numbers and bank information they gave you, so we can put a trace on the money and follow any subsequent transfers. We'll put a dozen agents, all computer experts and forensic accountants, to work tracking the names associated with the accounts and cross-referencing them with what we've already learned about the crime ring.

How will that help Grace?

We can use the information we get to pull up an address, a rap sheet, a vehicle registration or driver's license, a credit-card purchase...*anything* that can help us close in on where Grace might be. There is always the risk, however, that we'll lose the trail of the money, and we won't be able to recover it when this is over. We could wind up at a dead end with no useful information to help us rescue Grace.

Elise met Jared's gaze. "It sounds like a long shot, but we have nothing else."

"Are you all right with the idea of putting that much money on the line if it doesn't work?" he asked her, covering her hand with his.

She gave him a weak smile. "Like you said, it's just money, right? I'd do anything to get our little girl back."

Our little girl. Elise hadn't realized what she said until she saw the stunned and grateful warmth that lit Jared's eyes. She gave his fingers a return squeeze and drew a deep breath. "Let's do it."

Elise and Jared spent the next several minutes instant messaging with MysteryMom and her team, sharing the information the kidnappers had given them about how to make the payment and getting last-minute instructions on how and when to wire the money. Because she would be heavily involved in tracking the case herself, Mystery-Mom told them she might not be able to update them until everything had played out.

When she signed off, Elise and Jared looked at each other, the weight of the stress they shared unspoken but obvious.

"Well…" Jared said, lifting his cell phone to punch redial, "Here goes nothing. Or rather, here goes a quarter million."

Elise opened her mouth to thank him for his magnanimous gesture, but he turned his back as his broker answered.

"Yeah, Jared Coleman again. It's a go. Make the transfer to my savings account," he said into his cell phone as he strode across the room.

Elise felt the distance he put between them as a chill that sank into her bones. More than the loss of his physical presence beside her, she sensed a growing spiritual gap, as if he'd conceded defeat and was already withdrawing from her.

Could she blame him, after the heated words and bitterness they'd exchanged today? Had it all been today? It seemed eons ago she'd been dressing Isabel and found the birthmark on the girl's shoulder.

"I made lunch if anyone wants some," Michael said, coming back into the room with a plate of sandwiches.

Elise shook her head and lifted her cell phone to make her own call about transferring her savings to Jared's account, preparing for the payoff to the kidnappers. "If your offer of ten thousand is still good, Michael, we need it now."

Within minutes of the transfers reaching Jared's

account, MysteryMom's team had electronically wired the ransom payoff to the kidnappers. The hunt was on.

Within an hour, Michelle, Peter and Jared's parents had all arrived at Elise's house to join the vigil, waiting to hear from MysteryMom and lending their moral support to Elise and Jared.

Seeing the family's love and encouragement for Jared, Elise knew she'd made the right choice to let Jared retain custody of Grace. Her own brother tried to be supportive, but he was hit-and-miss at best. Grace deserved a big loving family, the family Elise couldn't give her.

She tried several times to speak to Jared about her decision, but with so many people in her tiny house, privacy was hard to come by. Finally, when he excused himself to retrieve a jacket from his car, Elise followed him outside, hoping for a couple minutes alone with him.

A light drizzle was falling, casting a gray pallor over the autumn afternoon, but Elise ignored the rain as she walked across her small lawn toward the curb where Jared had parked. He turned, his shoulders hunched against the rain, but straightened when he spotted her.

His face blanched, apparently mistaking her serious expression for an indication of bad news. "Elise, what is it? Did MysteryMom call?"

"No, I…just needed a chance to talk with you. Alone."

He held his hand out and tipped his face toward the sky. "And you chose here? In the rain?"

"There are too many people inside, and…" She licked the drops of rain from her lips and took a deep breath. "I wanted to thank you. For putting up so much money, all of your savings, to help bring Grace home."

He shook his head and lowered his gaze. "Don't thank me. It was no—"

She stepped close to him and covered his mouth with her hands. "Don't you dare say it was nothing! It was huge. And it showed me…" Her voice cracked, and she paused to clear her throat. "It brought home to me how very much you love Isabel."

He put a hand on each of her shoulders, and the gentle strength of his fingers sent ribbons of warmth through her. "Of course I love Isabel. Deeply. But that's not the only reason I did it."

Elise blinked as drizzle dripped from her hair into her eyes. "It wasn't?"

He shook his head and held her gaze. His dark eyes drilled to her core. "Beside knowing I couldn't live with myself if I didn't do everything in my power to save Izzy, I saw how much you were hurting, saw the depth of your agony and remembered everything you said about how Grace's death ripped out your heart. I couldn't let you suffer that again. I love you too much to see you hurt like that."

Elise caught her breath. "Wh—what?"

He stroked his hand along her cheek and captured her chin with his palm. "The other reason I gave all my money to save Isabel…to save *Grace*…is because I love *you*."

Elise tried to speak, but her voice was trapped behind the lump of emotions that clogged her throat.

"I know I should have said something before now." He lifted the corner of his mouth in a rueful smile. "Like when I proposed to you. I should have told you long ago how much you mean to me."

Tears joined the raindrops filling her eyes and tickling her cheeks. "But…I came out here to tell you I wasn't going to take Isabel away from you. I saw how much you loved her, and I could never hurt you that way." Her chest clenched. "Because… I love you."

He pulled his eyebrows into a dubious frown. "Wait, what? You're not going to fight me for custody?"

She wiped futilely at the moisture on her face. "No. Though…I'm hoping, praying, you'll be kind enough to allow me liberal visitation rights. I don't want to lose touch with her. Whether you tell her I'm her mother or not will be your choice."

He raked both hands through his wet hair and took a step back. He tipped his head back and shouted a laugh to the sky. "Elise, did you hear what I just told you? I love you." He seized her shoulders again, and the smile on his lips shone also from his eyes as he enunciated each word slowly. "I. Love. You."

Elise's pulse seemed to slow as realization dawned, and a bubble of hope expanded in her chest. "Jared, are you saying…"

"I still want to marry you. I want your courage and compassion and beauty and intelligence and loving heart in my life for always…" he paused, his face darkening "…even…even if we don't get Grace back."

Elise slammed her eyes shut and shook her head. "No! Don't even say that!" Now she pinned him with a hard, penetrating stare. "We can't think that way. We *can't!* MysteryMom's team *will* find her and bring her back. We have to stay positive."

He framed her face in his hands and brushed a kiss across her forehead. "Of course. You're right. My point is I would love you and want you for my wife, even if we didn't both love the same sweet baby girl with all our hearts."

Elise fought for a breath, joy filling her chest so completely there was no room for air. After a lifetime of rejection and betrayal, loss and disappointment, Jared was offering her an unconditional gift of love and acceptance. A future.

But what kind of future would they have if Mystery-Mom's agents couldn't find Grace in time?

Her fingers curled into the damp fabric of his shirt. "And if we don't get Grace back—"

"Shh!" He waved a hand, cutting her off. "We just said we weren't going to think that way."

Her grip on his shirt tightened. "I know, but…"

"Then I will stand by you and love you, and we will struggle through the loss together."

Together. No matter what life threw at her, she didn't have to be alone anymore. She nodded her head slowly, a tender ache flooding her heart, as tears of joy washed down her cheeks. "Yes."

He smiled and arched an eyebrow. "Yes…what?"

"Yes, I love you, and I will marry you."

An expression of bliss and relief crossed his face before a wide grin tugged his cheeks. Pulling her close and whispering her name, he captured her mouth with a deep, soulful kiss. As she wrapped her arms around his neck and leaned into the kiss, a sunbeam broke through the clouds and filled the sky with its buttery light.

The first purple shadows of evening had just begun to creep across Elise's yard when her phone trilled. Not a text-message beep, but a ring that meant someone was waiting to speak to her at the other end of the line.

The stir of conversations and idle activity in her living room ceased, and six pairs of eyes turned expectantly toward Elise as she lifted her cell phone from the coffee table to read the caller ID.

"Out of area," she reported, then cast an anxious glance to Jared. Fear crimped her gut, and her hand shook so hard, she nearly dropped the phone. "What if it's the kidnappers again?"

Jared moved to her side, circling her shoulders with his arm and giving her a reassuring squeeze. "Go on. Answer it."

She pulled in a cleansing breath and thumbed the answer button. "Hello?"

"Elise?"

The voice was a woman's. Elise's heart beat triple time. "Y-yes?"

"This is MysteryMom."

The whooshing of blood filled her ears, and a wave of panic knocked the air from her lungs. She'd never spoken to MysteryMom before. What did it mean that she'd chosen to call this time instead of messaging her or texting?

She tried to speak, but all that escaped her throat was a choked-sounding whimper.

"First and foremost," MysteryMom said, "we found Grace. She is safe, and she is unharmed."

Relief crashed through Elise so hard and fast that her head spun and her knees buckled. She slumped against Jared with a sob of joy.

"I just wanted to tell you that up front," MysteryMom said, "because I know how worried you've been."

Elise felt the shudder that rolled through Jared, and when she raised her gaze to him, his devastated expression told her he'd misinterpreted her reaction. Swallowing hard to clear the emotion tightening her throat, she smiled broadly and laughed. "No, it's good news! They found her, and she's okay!"

A cheer went up in the room, and Jared hugged her so tightly she could barely breathe. Michael beamed at her and sent her a wink.

MysteryMom was telling her something, but the buzz of excitement in the room and rush of adrenaline in Elise's ears drowned her out. She waved a hand at the room, signaling for quiet. "I'm sorry, can you repeat that?"

MysteryMom chuckled. "I know it's a lot to take in. In a nutshell, because of the information we gleaned while tracking the money transfers today, we were able to issue a warning to airports, bus stations and border crossings."

Elise tilted the phone so Jared could put his head close to hers and listen with her.

"We had a fuzzy picture from a security camera at an ATM in Laredo, Texas, taken when our kidnappers accessed the account where the ransom had ended up after several transfers. That fuzzy photo, along with the picture of Grace you provided, was sent out far and wide, and an alert guard at the Mexican border spotted Grace in the backseat of a Ford Taurus that had been reported stolen earlier in the day."

"Oh, thank God!" Elise pressed a hand over her heart and shivered, realizing how close the kidnappers had come to getting Grace out of the country. Had they gotten her into Mexico, the odds of ever recovering her would have been drastically reduced.

Jared apparently reached the same conclusion, because a half-relieved sigh, half moan rumbled from his chest.

Happy tears dampened her cheeks, and Elise swiped at them with the back of her hand. "Where is she now? How do we get her back?"

"She's in protective custody at the Laredo police department. They have a child-services agent on the way to move her to a more child-friendly location until you can get there. They won't reveal that location until one of you proves a legal claim to her, so be sure you both take a photo ID with you, and any legal documents showing your relationship with her. Oh, and there will be a bit of red tape to handle with the police and the bank, but Jared should be able to recover the ransom money in a few weeks."

Jared stepped away from their huddle over the phone, plowed both hands through his hair as he laughed, then gave his mother a big hug. In hushed tones, he repeated what they'd learned to their family, and Elise moved to a quiet corner of the room to finish the call.

"I...I don't suppose you have any information about a baby girl born to Greg and Kim Harrison at Crestview Memorial about six months ago? They were told their baby died under the same sort of odd circumstances as I was and...well, I was hoping..."

"Oh. Let me check the records," MysteryMom said, and Elise held her breath as she heard papers ruffling in the background. "Yes, here they are and...their baby...hmm, is apparently still at a Second Chance foster home. The adoptive parents they'd lined up backed out when a health problem was discovered with the baby."

Elise frowned. "What kind of health problem?"

"Deafness in one ear."

She sighed her relief. "Nothing life-threatening then, thank God. Have they been notified about their baby?"

"Don't know. But if they haven't been, they'll soon be. We're going through the files and parent notifications slowly but surely."

Her smile returned along with a sense of peace and deep gratitude. "How can I ever thank you enough for everything you've done? I'll happily pay whatever fee you charge for your services or—"

"Oh, stop!" MysteryMom said. "There's no fee. I do this because I want to, because it's my calling. My reward is in the happiness and relief I hear in your voice. The best way to thank me is to cherish every day with your daughter and give her a safe, loving and happy home to grow up in."

Elise looked to the celebration in her living room and smiled. "I can promise that. She will be surrounded with love and family."

"As for you…" MysteryMom said, "don't be afraid to open your heart to Grace's adoptive father. Life is too short to hold grudges, and he clearly has a lot of love to give… and not just to Grace."

Elise's heart warmed, and she met Jared's gaze across the room. "That I can promise, too."

Jared stepped away from the clamor of his family and moved toward her, grinning from ear to ear.

"In that case, I'll say goodbye, good luck and live well, Elise."

"You, too, MysteryMom. And thank you again from the bottom of my heart." She disconnected the call and fell into Jared's waiting arms. She angled her head to receive a deep kiss that tasted sweet with triumph and new beginnings. When they finally came up for air, Jared rested his forehead against hers and murmured softly, "So what do you say? Shall we go pick up our daughter?"

Our daughter.

Elise smiled and nodded. "I thought you'd never ask."

Epilogue

In her home office, MysteryMom rocked back in her desk chair and gave a satisfied sigh. Helping reunite baby Grace with her mother had been immensely gratifying work, especially since her associates had been able to bust up such a large crime ring, as well.

She rolled her computer mouse, clicking a few links to surf over to a chat room where another Grace, this one the mother of triplets, was waiting to hear from her.

Triplets! MysteryMom smiled and shook her head. Yes, as a single mom to triplets, Grace Sinclair had her hands full. What Grace needed was someone to share the job of parenting. And MysteryMom knew just where to start…

* * * * *

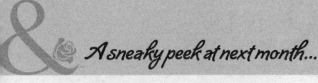

A sneaky peek at next month...

INTRIGUE...

BREATHTAKING ROMANTIC SUSPENSE

My wish list for next month's titles...

In stores from 18th May 2012:

☐ A Daughter's Perfect Secret – Kimberly Van Meter

& Lawman Lover – Lisa Childs

☐ Operation Midnight – Justine Davis

& A Wanted Man – Alana Matthews

☐ High-Stakes Affair – Gail Barrett

& Deadly Reckoning – Elle James

☐ Cowboy's Triplet Trouble – Carla Cassidy

Available at WHSmith, Tesco, Asda, Eason, Amazon and Apple

Just can't wait?

Visit us Online

You can buy our books online a month before they hit the shops! **www.millsandboon.co.uk**

0512/46

2 Free Books!

Join the Mills & Boon Book Club

Want to read more **Intrigue** stories?
We're offering you **2 more**
absolutely **FREE!**

We'll also treat you to these fabulous extras:

- 🌹 Books up to 2 months ahead of shops

- 🌹 FREE home delivery

- 🌹 Bonus books with our special rewards scheme

- 🌹 Exclusive offers... and much more!

Treat yourself now!

Visit us Online   Get your FREE books now at
www.millsandboon.co.uk/freebookoffer

0112/I2XEA/RE

MILLS & BOON
Book Club

2 Free Books!

Get your free books now at
www.millsandboon.co.uk/freebookoffer

Or fill in the form below and post it back to us

THE MILLS & BOON® BOOK CLUB™—HERE'S HOW IT WORKS: Accepting your free books places you under no obligation to buy anything. You may keep the books and return the despatch note marked 'Cancel'. If we do not hear from you, about a month later we'll send you 5 brand-new stories from the Intrigue series, including two 2-in-1 books priced at £5.49 each and a single book priced at £3.49*. There is no extra charge for post and packaging. You may cancel at any time, otherwise we will send you 5 stories a month which you may purchase or return to us—the choice is yours. *Terms and prices subject to change without notice. Offer valid in UK only. Applicants must be 18 or over. Offer expires 31st July 2012. **For full terms and conditions, please go to www.millsandboon.co.uk/freebookoffer**

Mrs/Miss/Ms/Mr (please circle) _____

First Name _____

Surname _____

Address _____

_____

_____ Postcode _____

E-mail _____

Send this completed page to: Mills & Boon Book Club, Free Book Offer, FREEPOST NAT 10298, Richmond, Surrey, TW9 1BR

Find out more at
www.millsandboon.co.uk/freebookoffer

Visit us Online

0112/I2XEA/REV

Book of the Month

MILLS & BOON

COWBOY'S TRIPLET TROUBLE

CARLA CASSIDY

BOOK OF THE MONTH

INTRIGUE...

We love this book because...

Dark, determined cowboy Jake fights against the odds to keep his newfound family safe in this pulse-racing romantic suspense from Intrigue sta Carla Cassidy.

On sale 18th May

Visit us Online

Find out more at
www.millsandboon.co.uk/BOTM

0512/BOTM

Special Offers

Every month we put together collections and longer reads written by your favourite authors.

Here are some of next month's highlights— and don't miss our fabulous discount online!

KASEY MICHAELS

THE TAMING OF THE RAKE

On sale 18th May

Summer Nights with a VAMPIRE

On sale 1st June

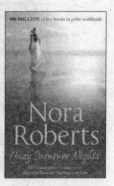

100 MILLION of her books in print worldwide

Nora Roberts

Hazy Summer Nights

On sale 1st June

Save 20%
on all Special Releases

Find out more at
www.millsandboon.co.uk/specialreleases

Visit us Online

0512/ST/MB375

Mills & Boon® Online

Discover more romance at
www.millsandboon.co.uk

- 🌹 **FREE** online reads
- 🌹 **Books** up to one month before shops
- 🌹 **Browse our books** before you buy

...and much more!

For exclusive competitions and instant updates:

 Like us on **facebook.com/romancehq**

 Follow us on **twitter.com/millsandboonuk**

 Join us on **community.millsandboon.co.uk**

Visit us Online   Sign up for our FREE eNewsletter at **www.millsandboon.co.uk**

WEB/M&B/RTL4